PART-TIME
Husband

Lovey LaRue

Blackstone LaRue

First Edition

LCCN: 2025905393

Paperback ISBN: 979-8-9926535-1-9

Digital ISBN: 979-8-9926535-0-2

Cover design by Hodel Crane Blackstone, Kathryn R. Biel, Jessica Martin-Bethard

Edited by V.H.Q. Blackstone, Jessica Martin-Bethard

Greetings Reader

Part-Time Husband is a slice of life, all fun and full of shenanigans, character-driven story. Our female main character deals with undiagnosed Autism, ADHD, and Anxiety. She is unaware and does not seek diagnosis or treatment in this book.

You will find spoilers for the movie The Last Holiday in Chapter 9. Don't worry, you'll see them coming.

Please be aware that the following potentially offensive material will be found within these pages:

Mild Drug Use

Alcohol Use

Graphic Sex Scenes

Raunchy Language

Inappropriate Jokes

Mild Violence

Thank you for reading my story and I hope you enjoy living life with Roni and Quinn as much as I have enjoyed creating that life.

With Love

For my husband,

I love you always, forever.

This might not be our love story but our love is woven throughout these pages.

Prologue

S haking the Polaroid, Rebecca hands it and the camera to me, smiling, before turning to Helen, "Congratulations! The opening went perfectly! We sold almost double what we expected! Not a bite of food left over, either. You guys want to head down to the diner? I'm starving, and their brunch is all I can think about. Jett and Sammy are already heading that way."

I look at Helen, her dark sepia skin glowing against her hot pink suit, deferring to her opinion since this was her big day. She grins at me. "Why don't we just pick up some food and head back to my place?"

"Whatever you want today, Sugar," I say, kissing her cheek.

Rebecca waggles her eyes at us and, after the goodbyes, leaves us standing on the sidewalk outside of my girlfriend's brand-new bookshop.

I secure an Uber, and we wait against the store's window.

"I want to ask you something," Helen says, looking at me nervously.

"Anything."

"Will you move in with me?"

"What?" I gasp, dread mounting in my chest. Damn it.

"I would like you to move in with me. We've been seeing each other for almost a year; if you count the months we were super casual. But we've been exclusive for six months. I think it's time we took this relationship to the next level." She says.

"But I told you, I don't do the next level. Helen, I can't move in with you." I say, my voice cracking, knowing that this is the end of Helen and I.

"You mean you won't. You won't move in with me. You won't truly commit to me. You've just been wasting my time. A fucking waste of time." She says quietly, with tears in her eyes.

My heart aches to see what this is doing to her, but I can't change who I am. I'm definitely not worthy of a woman as magnificent as Helen. I know that for a fact, I just hate that now she sees it, too.

"I'm sorry I was selfish and wanted to keep you for my own for just a little while. I'm so sorry," I say, knowing that won't make her feel any better.

"Keep your damn apologies," Helen says, patting under her eyes and straightening her shoulders. "I thought this was something. I thought your never-moving-in-together shit was just until you were sure."

"I'm sorry," I say again. I grab her hands, but she jerks away as the Uber pulls up. She doesn't even look at me as she stomps to the car, slamming the door and driving away.

My apartment isn't too far from here, so I walk home, needing time to clear my mind. But it doesn't work. Slowly, the fingers of claustrophobia grip my throat, making it hard to breathe. I'm tired of leaving, but I can't stay. I feel restless as if this city isn't big enough for me anymore. I reach my apartment, punch in my code, and hustle inside. My cat, a plump Siamese named Ginger, runs up to me, so I scoop her up and give her cuddles before depositing her on the table and sitting down. I google moving companies and cleaning services, get both lined up, and then pack. I'll be out the door with two bags, the cat and her accessories. I have to drop off my spare key to the movers and my main key to the cleaners and then Ginger and I can get out of New York City.

I take a moment to survey my apartment for the last time as my emotions bubble to the surface. Fuck, I do not have time for this, but the tears do not care. I rush into the bathroom, turn off the light, and sit on the toilet. Sobs wrack my body as flashes of Helen's face torture me. I never should have dated her. She was always too good for me. And then I hurt her? She was right. I'm not worthy, not worthy to even be in the presence of someone as magnificent as her. What did she even see in me? I'm broken, incapable of falling in love.

On and on, my thoughts spiral. Hatred of myself swirls in my head as I cry.

When I'm finally all cried out, I look into the mirror, taking in my messy blonde hair and red, puffy eyes, trying to find what Helen saw in me. I take a deep breath and splash water on my face.

It's time to go.

Just as I'm throwing the last of Ginger's shit into my Jeep, Helen walks up, "Where are you going?"

"I'm leaving, not sure where yet."

"You weren't even going to tell me."

"Didn't figure you wanted to hear from me."

"I was coming over here to make things right between us. I'm in love with you; we can make it work with two residences."

"Helen, baby, no. I can't do that to you. You deserve to have it all, and I can't give that to you."

"Wait, wait, you can't just leave!" Helen cries, gasping for air.

"I'm so sorry," I say again, for the last time, as I climb into the jeep and start the ignition. Ginger yells at me from her cat carrier, and I promise to stop in a few minutes to get her settled. I need to get away from Helen. I glance in the rearview mirror and see Helen standing there, tears running down her face.

The guilt threatens to swallow me whole, and I almost turn around. Just move right in with her to put a smile back on her face, but I would be miserable and make her miserable with me.

I stop at the gas station to fill up and pull into a parking spot to run inside for road snacks. I then settle Ginger into her car seat and pull out my phone. I feel so sad, anxious, and guilty. Maybe I just need to go home. I wait for that familiar claustrophobia to set in, as it does every time I think about going back home. But this time, a feeling of peace washes over me.

I press speed dial number 2 and wait for my brother, Brian, to answer. "Hey there, V-baby, what's up?"

"Can Ginger and I stay with you?"

"Of course, planning a vacation? We'd love to have you. Maybe we could get a condo at the beach for a week?"

"Um, that sounds great, actually. But not a vacation. I think I'm moving back home. I'm tired of traveling, and Helen, well, we broke up."

"Oh, baby, I'm sorry. I liked Helen."

"I did too"

"What happened?"

"She wanted to move in together, take our relationship to the next level. But I can't do that. She's in love with me. I can't stick around."

"You don't love her?"

"I love her like I love Rebecca and Jett and Sammy. But I'm not in love with her. I don't even think I have the capacity for that emotion."

"You just haven't met the right person yet."

"Sure, sure. Look, I'm fixing to drive your way. I don't have a plan, so I'll see you in a few days, maybe a week or two. I've turned that GPS app on so you can keep track of me."

"Ok, V-baby. I love you. See you when you get here. Keep me updated. I know I have that tracker but I want to hear from you that you're ok."

"Yes, sir. Love you too."

Chapter 1
Home ownership is bullshit.

Roni

"Fuck this shit." I snarl, holding up my yellow screen door with one hand and trying to get the hinges to line up so I can screw this damn thing where it belongs.

I never planned on owning a house.

Or settling down.

But after two decades of travel, living a nomadic lifestyle-it started to suck. And one thing my life does not do is suck.

I was settling down in New York, but when my ex and I broke up, the whole state felt too small. So I came home. Back to this teensy town in Alabama. Back to the woods and the rivers. The Spanish moss and pickup trucks. The thick accents, mosquitos, and the fantastic food. I wanted to be near my family, but not too near, so I found a lovely blue house way out in the woods, down a cute little dirt road, and bought it. And it came with a nice little guest house. That was a pleasant surprise. One of these days I'll find a renter but for now I'm using it for storage.

I've been home for a couple of years now, and home ownership is total bullshit. I fix myself another cup of tea and pick up my feline companion, Ginger, from the laptop so I can use it. I need to figure out how to have a house but not have to take care of a house. Perhaps I should hire a handyman to be on call? Or is there a service I can use? Damn it, all I know is that I don't want to pick up a single tool again.

I need a husband; that's what I need.

I shudder at the thought. I won't even let a stinky boy spend the night in my bed, much less let him live with me. His balls on my couch and feet on my coffee table? Absolutely not.

So, no husband. But husband-like, perhaps? A fellow that would be at my beck and call for non-sexual husbandly duties. Repairs, home improvement projects, catching and releasing critters, those sorts of things.

He can't be married. It feels disrespectful to spend time alone with a married man, and coordinating his partner's schedule with his is too much of a hassle.

Ok. I need a single man that won't want to screw up our working relationship by adding love or sex. Do I pay him? Of course, I pay him. How much? Then that brings me full circle to hiring a handyman of sorts.

Fuck.

Oh! Bachelors probably want home-cooked meals and a clean house. I can do that. Now that I've been home, I've found that I love cooking.

That would be perfect. A bachelor who has no interest in pursuing a relationship but would love the benefits of a wife while I get the benefits of a husband.

I take to my rarely used social media, clear out the overabundance of notifications, and type out my job offer.

I chuckle to myself. Job offer. Barter offer? That's hard to say.

I post my ad and close the computer. Well, that's that. I then wander out to my garden and start puttering around for a couple of hours, the husband hunt forgotten.

I fix myself a tomato sandwich, open the app, and find eighteen notifications.

Jesus Christ on a cranberry cracker.

Most of them are folks trying to find me a real husband.

My son would be perfect for you, he's 52 and lives at home...

I think my ex and you would hit it off, he's an amateur philosopher...

My friend Ray is looking for wife number three...

I'll introduce you to my neighbor, his wife left him last week...

My cousin just got out of prison...

I ignore those.

But the rest? They tagged a fellow, and he replied! He's interested in home-cooked meals—really interested. He's willing to submit a resume and references.

Oh, this is hilarious. I click on his profile to scope him out a bit.

Well, well, well. He's a hottie, isn't he? Big guy, kind face, looks like he works hard.

I send him a message and cross my fingers.

Quinn

I glance at my phone and notice I have a message from a mutual friend. Hoping it's the chick with the food, I open it.

Hell yeah.

It's her. She wants to know if I'm serious about being her 'part-time husband' and, if so, what kind of food I like.

Oh, hell yes.

I ask her to meet up with me somewhere so we can get to know each other and all that shit. We agreed to meet the next day at this tea place I'd never even heard of.

I text Kenny to see if he wants to meet me at Travis's, the local bar, and give me the details on this Veronica woman. Not trying to get myself wrapped up in some crazy woman's schemes. He says he'll meet me in about an hour, giving me time to kill. Kenny has been my best friend for close to 30 years, and his wife has known Roni since high school. If anyone would tell it to me straight, it's Kenny. Hell, if I had listened to him way back in the day, I probably wouldn't have a failed marriage under my belt.

I look around my bare one-bedroom apartment and wonder if it's time to buy a house. I'm 43 and have the money in the bank, and if this chick is serious, I'll have a wife-lady to clean it and bring me food.

I sit down to play the guitar until it's time to head out. Zoning out, strumming along, imagining all the home-cooked meals that might be in my future. I wonder if she can do pies, I'd be willing to actually marry her for a damn cherry pie.

I don't even want to get married again, but for a good pie, maybe. Or cookies. Biscuits. Fried chicken.

Shit, it's a miracle that none of my exes tricked me into marriage with food. A baby, sure. I wish she had shown me a picture of a pie instead of an ultrasound. Shaking away that nasty train of thought, I glance at the clock and see it's about time to head to the bar. I hop on my bike and make it to Travis's Bar at the same time as Kenny.

Other than our similar t-shirt and jeans, Kenny is practically my opposite in looks. He is a good foot shorter than I am, thin where I am thick, with big glasses and a thin mustache. He has skin prone to freckles and reddish-blonde hair.

We man-hug, which is really just a bunch of slapping on the back, and go inside the nondescript building, made interesting by its fire engine red color.

"I swear this door gets heavier every time we come here," Kenny complains, tugging the thick wood door open. The faint smell of smoke from decades past, mixed with the stronger smell of beer, washes over us as we walk to the bar in the back under a slew of neon signs. It's busy tonight with all the dark wood tables and most of the red leather booths taken. I clap Kenny on the back, "I'm going to grab us a booth. Get me my usual, alright?"

"Got it," He says.

I walk straight to the last empty booth, narrowly avoiding couples two-stepping around the darkened dance floor. Looking around, my eyes skim over the familiar wood paneling covered with metal automotive signs, license plates, and hubcaps.

Kenny makes it to our booth, beers in hand, but I start the questions before he can even get comfortable.

"Alright, what's up with this Veronica chick? Crazy? A bitch? A psycho killer? A perfectly nice lady that wants me to do the upkeep on her house?"

Kenny laughs and says, "Yeah, the last one for sure. But kind of the other ones, too. Though I don't think she's killed anyone yet. I wouldn't put it past her."

"That's...reassuring," I say, drinking my beer.

"Nah, she's a great gal. Rhonda loves her. Remember when Sarah May was born, and you ate all that casserole and pasta salad you swore you didn't like?"

"Oh, my God. She made those? I might have to make her wife number two."

Kenny laughs like I told the funniest joke in the world.

"What is so funny? I like food." I say, patting my stomach, which hasn't had an ab in about 20 years.

"Roni would never marry you." He says, around his laughter.

"Ouch. What's wrong with me?"

"Do you really want me to answer that? Kidding, dude. But seriously, Roni is never getting married. She's said, way too many times, how she doesn't want a dude's balls on her couch. She's really particular about her things."

"Uptight, is she?"

"Not at all, except in her own home. It's just a thing with her; she is super laid-back everywhere else," He says, still chuckling.

"Against marriage, might murder me, and doesn't want my balls on her couch? Sounds like my type."

"Come to think of it, you and Roni will probably get along great. Y'all both have a, what did Rhonda call it?" Kenny looks at me as if I know whatever word his wife had used. I shrug at him and wait for him to find the word.

"Quirky! Y'all both have a quirky sense of humor." He says triumphantly.

"I'm not quirky! I barely know what quirky even means." I say with a laugh.

"You think ridiculous things are funny. Roni is a ridiculous thing," He says, a thoughtful look on his face. "Shit, maybe this isn't such a good idea. Rhonda commented on y'all being perfect for each other, but I didn't really consider it. I don't want to see you hurt, especially if Rhonda and I gotta pick sides or some shit."

"Why would it be me getting hurt? You aren't worried that I would hurt Roni?"

"Nah, man, you're as loyal as they come. Hell, you stayed married to a raging bitch for way too long, and Roni isn't a raging bitch.

Roni, though, has a history of being flighty. She's pretty settled now, but who knows if this is permanent?"

"Look, I ain't aiming to fall in love or anything like that. I am just out to secure home-cooked meals."

"Alright, man, keep it that way. This one isn't about to let anyone wife her up."

"Actually, she's letting me part-time wife her up," I say, laughing way too hard at my own joke.

"Shut up."

Chapter 2
Magical Giggle

Roni

After I make plans with that Quinn fellow, I pour myself a cup of tea and look for Ginger. Finding her in the sunroom lounging in the papasan chair, I slide myself next to her and remember that I was supposed to video call my best friend, Val. Damn, I don't have my phone or tablet near me. I piss Ginger off as I get up to find my electronics; she hisses and runs under a plant stand. She takes a swipe at my leg as I walk by, the little rascal. Finding my phone by the tea kettle, I sit at the kitchen table and make the call. Looking around, I try to remember where I sat my tea.

They answer, their blonde pixie in disarray, with perfect makeup. I say, "So, I did a thing."

"Oh my glob, what did you do?" They ask, a grimace scrunching up their perfect hot pink lipstick.

"I might have caught myself a husband."

"What the hell? I'm on my way. Maybe there is a direct flight to Pensacola or Mobile leaving tonight. Shit." I watch them look around and grab random things to shove in a tote bag.

"Wait," I say, laughing, "A part-time husband."

"That doesn't reassure me in any way that you are ok," Val says, bright blue eyes glaring at the screen while tossing random items in the bag.

"Ok, so you know how I kind of hate owning a house, but I also love my house?"

"Yeah," Val says, rotating their hand in a circle to signal that I need to get to the point.

"Fine. So, I don't want to deal with any of the bullshit associated with home ownership. I had to fix my own screen door this morning. I did not like that at all. So I want someone who will be at my beck and call, who will come and fix my door, build a bat house, and get Ginger out of a tree. I didn't want to hire a guy because I would have to hire multiple guys, you know? The critter catcher isn't the same guy that will look at why my toilet is leaking."

"Wait, Ginger got stuck in a tree? And your toilet is leaking? And you have bats? I think I need to come home. Jesus Christ on a cranberry cracker. You are going through it."

I laugh, "You know Ginger can not climb a tree with her little fat ass. And no, I don't have bats, which is a problem. I kind of want bats. Did you know they are great pest control? And with my garden, they would be super beneficial. And my toilet isn't leaking, but what if it was? Stop distracting me. I'm telling you about my potential part-time husband. So I asked on social media if there was a confirmed bachelor that wants to trade doing all the shit I don't want to do for a clean house and home-cooked meals. Hence, the part-time husband deal."

"Ok. That sounds ridiculous. I love it." Val laughs.

"It is absolutely ridiculous. But if this works out the way I think it will, it's going to be great."

"Or you're going to get murdered by a strange man who has keys to your house."

I laugh and say, "I've got a guard cat; I ain't scared. So what's new with you? How's Memaw?"

"She's alright, I think. Got some guy working for her. Oh! Did I tell you about my date last week?"

"No, you didn't. I'm intrigued."

"Yeah, I swear he was a serial killer. Beady little eyes and greasy hair. I'm not entirely sure how I ended up on a date with him. I met him at a bar, but I think I was way more drunk than I realized," Val says with a chuckle.

"Jesus Christ on a cranberry cracker, you're worried about my potential part-time husband, but you are dating a serial killer!"

"I'm not dating him. I went on one date. He told me about some podcast he listened to, and I couldn't do it. I just stood up and left with him hollering after me. It was hilarious," Val laughs.

"Be careful. Maybe come home so I can make sure you are alive."

"We'll see," Val says mysteriously.

Quinn

No wonder I'm not familiar with this place, I think with a chuckle. I feel like a bull in a china shop, literally, with my massive frame in this tiny cafe with all sorts of breakables lining the walls.

I step outside to wait. Seems like the safest option. I pull up her profile and glance at her picture to recognize her upon arrival. Damn, she's gorgeous. Long dark blonde hair that looks barely tamed in a braid, glittering green eyes surrounded by laugh lines, and full lips made for smiles - Stunning. I click through her photos to see a woman who doesn't share much, but there are a handful that she's been tagged in. One shows this gorgeous woman standing with a couple of teenagers down in Gulf Shores. She's wearing a barely there bikini that shows her soft stomach and heavy breasts. The dimples on her thighs are just about the cutest thing, and I want to lick them.

Shit.

No.

She's off-limits.

Get it together.

Pretend you aren't a damn 16-year-old masquerading as a 43-year-old construction worker.

You are an adult.

Not ruled by your dick.

She's off-limits.

Not going to mess up a good thing of home-cooked meals for a quick lay.

Even if she is exactly my type.

She's probably a man-hating bitch, anyway. Why else would she want this sort of relationship?

My thoughts stutter to a stop when I see her getting out of the driver's side of an older orange jeep. A flowery dress covered by a dark purple cardigan and combat boots. Her dark blonde hair is loose and a little wild. God, I hope she's a raging bitch, or I'm in so much trouble.

"Quinn?" She asks with a raspy, smoky voice while thrusting her hand out.

"Yup. Veronica?" I ask back while shaking her hand.

"Call me Roni, please. Wanna grab a tea, and we can sit and chat?"

"Alright, Roni. Could we sit outside? I feel like I'm going to Hulk smash that place just by sneezing or something."

Her giggle sounds like magic.

Magic? Shit, I've lost my damn mind.

"Sure, we could grab drinks and go sit over by the train." She says, gesturing across the street where there is a train museum and decommissioned trains that kids love to climb around on.

"Absolutely." I grin and offer her my arm.

Shut up.

I can do that. She is going to be my part-time wife, after all.

Inside I immediately hit my head on a low-hanging basket chandelier-type thing. I just know I am going to break something in here.

Luckily, Roni didn't see anything and turned to hand me a tea menu.

Black tea. Green tea. Oolong tea. And so on. And on. And on. How many tea combinations could there possibly be? According to this menu, probably a billion. I've only ever had sweet tea, and none of this shit is that.

"Ok, I've never even considered a tea that doesn't start with the word sweet. What should I get?"

"Oh!" She exclaims and then asks all sorts of tea questions I have no answer to, so I interrupt her and say, "Maybe just order me whatever you're getting as long as it's sweet?"

Another magical, ahem, regular - just regular- giggle, and she says, "Of course."

After acquiring our teas, we make our way across the grass to where the train is, only to find that a child's birthday party has taken over the picnic tables.

I open my mouth to suggest we head over towards the clock tower and fountain when she says, "Here, hold my tea, and I'll go grab a blanket from the truck, and we can sit under that tree if that's ok with you?" After I agree, she does a little jog-walk to her Jeep and returns with an old patchwork quilt that has seen better days.

"Let me just shake the sand out of it. I forgot to wash it after my beach trip last week." She says, shaking debris out of the ratty blanket.

We settle in, and she looks at me expectantly. "How's the tea?"

I take my first sip and must do a poor job of covering my dismay because she laughs and says, "I'm sorry! I thought having them add extra sugar would make it work for you!" and then she sips her tea and exclaims, "Gross! This one's yours!" while making a gagging face. She snatches the tea from my hand and takes a swig, "Oh yeah. This one is mine. Here, this one is practically all sugar."

I hesitantly take a sip.

Ok, I can get behind this one. It's not as good as a Mawmaw's sweet tea, but it's pretty tasty.

"So," I say as I get comfortable on the blanket, "Why this part-time husband arrangement? Trying to bring back the barter system?"

Her loud, snorting laugh is not magical, but it makes me laugh with her.

"Not exactly. I just want more personalized service than a handy-man. I want someone who will do the little things like catch a critter in my house, and then check the toilet, then cut down a tree or something. I don't want to call 12 different people to find some help. Like, the other day I was trying to fix my screen door. I can do it, but I simply do not want to. That was the first time I thought 'I need a husband', which was horrifying. A gross, stinky man in my cute little home?"

She delicately shudders before continuing, "No thanks. But that's why I wanted a confirmed bachelor. Someone who isn't going to want to marry me but doesn't have other home-type obligations."

"You don't like men? Not looking for a bed-warmer that can do upkeep on your house?"

She laughs that magical laugh again, "Absolutely not. I dig men well enough, but I live alone. I have no desire for cohabitation."

The way she says 'cohabitation" makes me laugh out loud at the disgust on her face.

"So," she says with a grin, "Want to give it a go?"

"Maybe," I smirk. "How's your cooking and cleaning? Kenny informed me that I've had your amazing casserole and pasta salad, but those could be a fluke. I want real food. I've considered proposing marriage to Dora at the Waffle House after tasting her fried chicken at a church potluck. I'm pretty sure she'd say yes."

She snort-laughs in the cutest way possible and says, "I suppose you have a really hard choice to make. Especially since Dora's 65th birthday is next week. That's a big one and I'm sure you haven't gotten her a gift yet. Mr. Jeff has been sweet on her for a few months now, so you'll have to do better than him at gift-giving if you want to lure her away."

"Well, hell, woman. Looks like I'm stuck with you."

There's that laugh again.

"Ok, I'll tell you what. Get up with me this weekend. I should be home, and I'll cook you dinner. You can come over, I'll show you around, we'll eat and discuss this arrangement. What do you want me to make you?"

"Oh, shit. Really? Anything?" I ask excitedly.

"Just about it. I'm not professionally trained, just Memaw trained, you know?"

"Fuck. Yeah. Fried chicken, collards, cornbread? No. Biscuits? Cornbread, for sure."

"I'll do biscuits and cornbread, just for you, and how about some black-eyed peas? I froze some a couple of months back that turned out so good. And a fruit pie? I have cherries, blueberries, and apples put up."

This is the moment that I know I will do anything this woman asks, just so she will cook for me.

"Woman, I haven't had a homemade cherry pie since my Gigi passed some 20 years ago. And if this food is anything as good as it sounds, I will do whatever you ask me to."

"That's what I'm hoping for." She says with a saucy wink.

Chapter 3
Half full teacups & Crocs.

Roni

The cold water is a shock to my system as I try to rinse the dirt from my hands. Well, at least enough to check my phone. Wiping the grime down the leg of my overalls I grab my phone and notice that the text is from Quinn.

Hey, could I come over today to check out your house?

A strange excitement flutters over me and I think about how much time I would need to shower and get ready.

Wait.

No.

This is not a date. I'm not trying to impress him. I'll tell him to come over now, that'll set the tone for our absolutely not romantic relationship.

Yeah, come over whenever. I'm out working in the yard, so if I don't answer the door just walk around back.

I press send before I change my mind.

He replies almost immediately.

Cool. Be there in about 15 minutes.

Fuck.

* * *

———◆◇◆———

Quinn

I'm confused as I pull into her drive. She said she lived all alone 'out in the woods,' but there is another house right across the dirt driveway from what I am hoping is hers. Dude, what if I managed to get lost and this isn't her place? I'm going to get shot by some shotgun-toting guy with a farmer's tan and a beer belly, aren't I?

Oh, no, I'm good. I see her orange jeep peeking around the side of the light blue house as I take my helmet off and shove it in my saddlebag. Is that Paradise by the Dashboard Light I hear? I decide to follow the music around to the back of the house instead of trying the front door first.

Roni is up to her elbows in dark dirt, her pink overalls covered in debris as she finishes potting a very dangly plant. She hasn't noticed me yet, and the woman's part of the song is coming up, so as I walk towards her, I belt out, "Stop right there..." and she startles and lands backward on her ass in the dirt as Meatloaf prays for the end of time. Veronica starts to snort-laugh as I rush over to pull her up.

"Well, hello there," I say with a chuckle once she is steady on her feet.

"Hi." She giggles, "Come on over here, and we'll get the dirt off, and I'll show you the place."

"I'm not sure I want to see it if it's anything like your shoe choices."

Veronica kicks off her lime green crocs with a chuckle "Shut up. They're hideous but the best thing to work in the garden in. And I can just hose them off if they get too gross!"

"Ok, ok. If you insist."

We enter her home through the back sunroom, with an emerald-patterned floor and a matching ceiling. She has wall-to-wall hanging plants, standing plants, and a cozy papasan chair with a banged-up end table sporting a stack of books and a half-full tea cup perched wobbly. It's earthy and cluttered and seems like it suits Roni but I would go nuts if I lived here. I prefer clean, simple spaces where you can actually see the walls.

Through the double glass doors, we enter her living room jungle. I'm overwhelmed with the sheer amount of things she fits in one room.

A deep purple overstuffed sofa was against one wall covered in about 3 multicolored crocheted throws, a double papasan chair stuffed with pillows in all sorts of colors and soft blankets was situated under a large window that you could barely see for all of the hanging plants and vines. Tiny tables dotted the whole room, two on either side of the sofa and papasan plus two on either side of the double doors and another by the front door. Most of those had books stacked on top and there was an alarming amount of half-full teacups scattered on any flat surface without a care for the precarious nature of it all. Five bookcases of various sizes and shapes overflowing with books filled in any empty areas this room might have had. Soft-looking rag rugs covered most of the hardwood floors and multiple floor pillows were haphazardly displayed in the corner.

Roni says "This is the living room, every so often I get a wild hair and decide to rearrange this mess and that is where you would come in, part-time husband."

"Whew," I whistle out, "Your cooking better be good, woman."

"Oh, it is. Come on."

She leads me into the kitchen and it is exactly like I would have expected. Drying herbs and flowers hanging from the ceiling, a scratched-up kitchen table with a chipped bowl of fruit in the center, bright handmade placemats, and mismatched chairs all around. An open pantry sat against the wall filled with home-canned fruits and vegetables. Wicker baskets filled with miscellaneous kitchen items, from utensils and dishes to containers of tea, sitting on all sorts of surfaces. A deep farmhouse sink sits under the bright window and she has tons of counter space, though a lot of it was holding her appliances. I notice that there are no cabinets, but there are another couple of half-full teacups. Wonder what's up with that?

"Hey, what's the deal with the cups everywhere? I swear you have like thirty teacups scattered throughout the house." I chuckle.

"Sometimes I forget I have a cup of tea and make a new one. It's not a big deal and definitely not thirty of them." She snaps at me as she grabs the cups.

"Shit, sorry. Didn't realize it was a sore subject."

"Sorry," she grumps. "I'm just really not used to anyone critiquing my space. I don't like it, hence the whole no person ever living with me deal." She finishes with a rueful laugh.

"No worries, if I spent that much time in my place I'd probably be the same way. Shit, speaking of, what's the deal with that other house? I thought you lived alone out here."

"Oh, I do. This house came with that one as a mother-in-law suite, but it's a whole ass house. One bedroom, one bath. Decent amount of space. I'm using it for storage right now."

Seeing an opportunity to get out of my bleak apartment and into the country, I say, "If you decide you dig me, could I interest you in renting it to me?"

She nods while looking thoughtful. "OK, I'll rent it to you. I can already tell that we are going to get along and having you right across from me would be super convenient. Besides, if it turns out you totally suck, I'll kick you out after a year."

"Seriously? Just like that?"

"Of course. I wouldn't hesitate to kick you out if you annoy me." She smiles at me.

"Oh hush, you. You know I meant me renting from you."

"Well, why not?"

Why not indeed?

Roni

Once I find the key to the other house, we walk across the yard. I toss him the key to let him in as I check the plants on the porch. I'll have to have my new part-time husband haul them back to my yard. I doubt he wants to care for them.

"What are you going to do with all the stuff in here?" He yells from inside the house. Damn, I didn't think about where to put all of my shit. I jog up the stairs and through the door to see him squatting down, looking under the kitchen sink. Damn, that's an ass, encased in soft faded denim and shoulders that are barely contained in his black t-shirt. He has a working man's body, soft but strong, no gym for this fellow. Oh, no. This man obviously does a hard job and loves good food. His thick middle and barrel chest make me want to climb in his lap and do naughty things. I'm a tall woman at 5'10 and he makes me feel small. Add in his brown hair that glints auburn in the sunlight and those killer brown eyes, thick beard and whew, I'm going to have some eye candy right next door.

"I don't suppose you want to build me a shed instead of the first month, last month, and security deposit, yeah?" His warm eyes crinkle at the corners as he chuckles.

"Yeah, that sounds perfect. What kind of shed? Just storage, keep the rain out, or like a tricked-out babe cave? I can do either, no problem."

"Babe cave?" I laugh, "Nah, my whole house is my babe cave, maybe somewhere in the middle. I want one with AC since I don't want to sweat balls trying to find something in there."

"Sounds good. Do you want me to have it finished before I move in?"

"As long as you don't care about sharing your space with my junk, you are welcome to move in tomorrow if you want."

"Awesome. So, um, about this dinner I was promised..."

I laugh as I lead him back to my house.

Quinn

I am so glad this woman doesn't want to get married.

If she did, I would have to marry her.

Fried chicken, collards, black-eyed peas, fried okra, cornbread, and biscuits. And a cherry pie. I'm stuffed and in heaven.

"I can't believe I ate that much." I groan as I lean back in my chair, "The only place I eat this good is at my Momma's, and she only cooks once a month since it's just her and dad. Thank you. I'll handle the dishes."

"Not this time. You're still a guest. Next time, you'll be my part-time husband, and I'll expect you to do the dishes if I've cooked." She says with a laugh, "Now come on, take a look around. Ask the questions."

We walk into her living room, and she leans over and scoops up a Siamese cat with a rather large behind, saying, "This is Ginger. She is like a sour patch kid, a sweet angel baby one minute and claws out the next."

"Nice to meet you," I say, scratching the cat's head. Good, I get sweet.

"The fact that you talk to animals like they're people bodes well for our relationship."

I grin at her as I roam around her home, finding myself staring at a wall of Polaroids that all feature Roni.

"So, want to take me down memory lane? Who are all these fellows in the photos?" I ask as I gesture to her wall of love past. "How many broke your heart and how many hearts did you break, my dear?"

Her magical giggle twinkles around the room, easing my inappropriate jealousy. Jealousy that I don't even understand. Shit, we are practically strangers in a symbiotic relationship. I bury those thoughts in the back corner of my brain to worry about later.

"You're really interested?"

"I asked, didn't I, woman?" I smirk at her.

"Fine, fine." She rolls her eyes pointing to a picture of a younger her in an old-fashioned black dress with her arms around a similarly dressed young man with dark hair. They are standing in front of a massive house and laughing into each other's eyes. "This is Ricco, and we were both tour guides at the Winchester Mystery House. That was so much fun, I had been obsessed with it since I was like 5 years old and saw it on an episode of Unsolved Mysteries." She says with a giggle. I want to ask about Ricco, did she love him? But I restrain myself.

She points to the next picture of her and a laughing dark-haired woman laying on a blanket on the beach with the ocean and cliffs in the background. That same woman shows up in quite a few photos. "This is Ezie. We were about 25 years old there. I met her while I was a tour guide at the Lizzie Borden house in Massachusetts. She came in for a tour and left me her number, along with a tip. I think we spent about six months together before fizzling out."

"You dated her?" I ask, a touch more aggressively than I intended.

Roni raises an eyebrow. "Yes, is that a problem?"

The laugh I let out isn't nervous, at least I hope it doesn't sound that way when I say, "No! Just unexpected, though I'm not sure why."

She laughs as she says, "No worries, I'm used to it. Apparently, I look like I only like dick, but that just isn't the case. Speaking of a dick..." she trails off as she gestures to another picture, this one showing a very ripped, tan, glistening fuck boy looking guy with blonde highlights holding a surfboard with his arm loosely across a windblown Roni's shoulders. Her tiny hot pink bikini glows neon against her pale skin and her shoulders, nose, and cheeks are a little red from the sun. I feel a bit creepy ogling a 20-something-year-old Roni, but she still looks practically the same, so I'm just ogling Roni, right? That's less creepy. Totally.

I force a laugh out and ask, "Was he as big of a douche as he looks?"

"Oh my glob, yes. Maybe bigger." She says, chuckling. And with that, she goes down the line from Roswell to Salem to Los Angeles and New York City. She traveled the country working cool jobs and meeting people worth hanging on her walls long after the last time she saw them. The last picture shows her looking just as she does now, with wild blonde hair and bright green eyes, wearing a pair of jeans with roses trailing up them and a lacy tank top holding the hand of a stern-looking black woman with dark shiny hair, a sleek pantsuit, and a small smile. The women are standing in front of a trendy shop looking like total opposites.

"That was my last day in New York. Helen owns the bookstore there. Just after this picture, she invited me to move in with her and I just couldn't. I can't imagine living with anyone, plus I wasn't in love with her. I thought about it, though. But it never would have worked out and she would have been more hurt the longer I stayed. She took it hard, and I just left. Grabbed the cat and whatever could fit in my jeep and came on home."

"Just like that? You packed up and left your whole life?" I ask incredulously.

"Oh, yes. I've done it so many times before. As long as I have Ginger, I'm good to go. I hire a moving company to pack my shit and a cleaning company to take care of the rest. I don't get attached to places. Even this house, I could just go, if I wanted to. Never come back and I'd be fine with it. Don't get me wrong, I love this house and living here. I don't have any plans of leaving, but..."

"That's really kind of incredible. Being able to just leave everything behind."

She chuckles sadly. "Yeah, tell that to Helen."

Chapter 4
That sounds like a threat.

Roni

A s I'm finishing up dinner I peer out the window and see Quinn's truck in his driveway. I don't think he's moved his stuff in yet, or at least, I didn't see him do it, so I text Quinn and see if he wants to come have dinner over here or if he wants me to bring him a plate. When there's a knock on my door less than a minute after sending the text, I didn't expect Quinn to be standing there. But he is.

"Hey, I would love to have dinner over here. I don't have any furniture in the house except for my bed. Some buddies and I will be bringing it all over tomorrow. Is dinner ready? I'm starving." He says, practically sniffing around me as he peers inside. I laugh and tell him, "Yes, dinner is ready. Go wash up, and I'll plate it out."

"Yes, ma'am!" He says, doing a little salute.

When he emerges, I have our plates ready with hamburgers, french fries, and a salad. He grins as he rubs his hands together and exclaims, "Oh my god. Homemade French fries? Woman, are you sure you don't want to get married? I swear I'll drop to one knee if you keep feeding me like this."

I laugh and say, "That sounds like a threat."

"Maybe it is," He says, laughing.

I tell him to have a seat, and he does as I sit his plate in front of him.

"You sure you don't want more? You cooked; I'm not trying to snatch food out of your mouth." He says, looking at his overflowing plate compared with my more modest portions.

I laugh, "Nope. I made this much just for you."

"You are an absolute angel."

We spend the next hour chit-chatting. He tells me stories of owning a construction company, and I thrill him with more tales from the road. He tells me all about his parents and sisters. I love hearing how close he is with them all, even though thinking of my parents brings up feelings of restlessness and sadness.

"What about your folks? Y'all close?" Quinn asks.

"With my siblings, yes. I'm the youngest of seven, and my oldest sister raised me after my parents died."

"Shit, woman. I'm sorry about your parents. Were you very young?" He asked.

"I was fourteen, so young enough. Left me feeling so unsettled and unstable. Like nothing in life is permanent."

Ginger weaves between our feet, meowing her displeasure over not being given a hamburger. As I lean over to scratch behind her ears, I realize he hasn't said anything about his personal life, about why he never wants to get married.

"So, how many ex-wives do you have hidden away so that you can promise me you won't go getting hitched and leave me all by myself to handle this damn house?" I ask as I clear our plates, put them into the sink, and start a pot of coffee.

"Just the one, and let me tell you, she's enough."

My chest feels like it's on fire. An ex-wife? He's been married. Why do I even care?

"Want to share the dastardly details since I've told you my life story?" I ask, halfway hoping he'll decline. The idea of him with a woman is oddly uncomfortable.

"Sure, it's the usual story. I dated Amanda all through high school. After graduation, she told me she was pregnant, so I did what you're supposed to do when you knock up your girlfriend, and I proposed. She wanted to get married before she started showing, so we did. But just after the little wedding, she confessed she had never been pregnant. She was just tired of waiting for me to propose. She didn't want to go to college or work. She wanted to be a stay-at-home wife. So she thought tricking me was the way to go. I was so pissed, almost filed for divorce right then, three weeks after our wedding. But I didn't. God, I wish I had. I gave up college to take a good-paying construction job, and we bought a little one-bedroom house. Then, she was so different after we bought the house. She would scream and throw things and try to keep me from seeing my friends. She spent every cent that wasn't for our bills and then complained that I never took her out. She made my life a nightmare."

Eyes wide, I say, "Holy fucking shit-balls, Quinn. That's crazy."

He nods, "Now, at eighteen, I'm sure I wasn't the best husband. I treated her well enough, especially in the beginning, but once she flipped the switch, I just know I was an asshole that just made everything worse. The final straw was when she demanded that I stay home, but I needed to get away from her, so I crashed at Kenny's for a few days. When I came home, all three of my guitars were smashed. One of those had been my grandfathers, who taught me to play. I filed for divorce the next day. Amanda got a good lawyer and blindsided me. She ended up getting our house and alimony, which just ended two years ago when she finally remarried. I know she did that shit on purpose to keep taking my money. She's had numerous live-in boyfriends in the last twenty years but never married. Every time I saw her around town, she had a smart comment about me buying her gas or groceries or whatever she was doing. Made my blood boil. And hell, if she wasn't trying to get me pissed off, she was trying to get back in my life. She didn't want me, but she damn sure didn't want me with anyone else. Never mattered to her I wasn't interested. She was determined to have me on the back burner."

"Fucking ducks, that's awful. No wonder you're soured on marriage. Hell, I'm soured on marriage just hearing this story. Do you need a hug or something?" I say, a little stunned that someone would treat a jolly fellow like Quinn that way. Though there are always two sides, but fuck, faking a pregnancy to trap someone in marriage? That's messed up.

"You know what, maybe I do need a hug. Wanna sit on my lap, too?" Quinn says, wiggling his eyebrows.

"Oh shush, you dreadful man. I can't believe I'm letting you live next door." I laugh, flicking the water off my wet hands toward his face.

"No take-backs! You're stuck with me!" He laughs like a cartoon villain while wiping the water droplets off his jaw.

Quinn

I hear music coming from Roni's backyard so I head over there to figure out where she wants her storage shed. And to discuss size and style. I'm excited about getting her junk out of my dining room. I walk around the corner and see her sitting on her back porch tying knots in rope, I think. I jog around and up her stairs. "Whatcha up to, Buga-loo?"

Her magical giggle fills the air as she says, "Making macrame keychains, Quinn Carl Evans! Let me see your keyring, please."

"Carl? That's not my middle name." I say with a chuckle as I pull my keys out of my pocket and toss them to her.

"Well, what is your middle name?" She asks, wrinkling her nose at my basic key set up of keys and a blue carabiner. She turns to the small pile of macrame keychains next to her and selects one that has a hot pink bead in it, then puts my keys on it. It doesn't matter to me what holds my keys together, but Carl as a middle name is offensive.

"I don't think I want to tell you since you thought it was Carl. Maybe you just have to keep guessing."

"Oh, fun! Here you go, Quinn Wyatt," she says, giggling, handing back my key set with its snazzy new macrame keychain.

"Not even close, dollface." I laugh when she wrinkles her nose, either at the endearment or at being told she's wrong.

"What are you making these for?" I ask.

"Fun," she shrugs, "I like doing macrame in small projects, so I just make a bunch of keychains or plant hangers and give them away. I think everyone I've ever met has at least 3 macrame things from me. Watch out, I'll have your house decorated in tiny macrame in no time."

I laugh, "Go right ahead, pretty girl. I don't have anything decoration-related, so if you want to toss some rope on my walls and shove a plant in them, it's all you."

"Oh goodie! So what brings you to my neck of the woods, husband? I doubt you sensed a new keychain in your future."

"Correct. I'm going to make your bitch barn today, need to know the who, what, when, where of it all," I say.

"Bitch barn? I think I prefer Babe Cave. Um. OK. Follow me," she says, putting all her macrame-making things in a bright green tackle box. She walks across her yard, about halfway between her house and the woods, and she stops.

"Here. I want it here."

"Alright, how big and what style?" I ask, pulling out my little notebook and a tape measurer.

"OK, so I am thinking about from here to here," she says, walking about 10 feet from her starting point, then points to a tree about 20 feet from where she now stands, "and a few feet in front of that tree."

"Alright, let me measure," I say as she continues to chatter on.

"I want it to have a pointy roof with cute curved shingles, and that swirly molding on the outside. And could you paint it yellow? And maybe repaint my doors to match it? That would be so cute!"

"So, you want a 10x16 gingerbread cottage-style shed painted yellow and your doors painted yellow. What color do you want the trim? And the door on the shed? Blue?"

She squeals and bobs her head to silent music and says, "Yes! The same color as the house!"

"Of course. Is there anything else?" I ask, grinning at her exuberance. I am thrilled with this arrangement; she is going to be an absolute blast to hang around with.

"Not that I can think of, but if you think of something super cute, do it!"

"I'm not a great judge of cuteness, but I'll do my best. Keep your phone on you and I'll text if I have questions." I say as I shove my notebook into my back pocket.

"Perfect!"

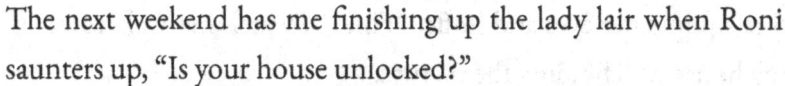

The next weekend has me finishing up the lady lair when Roni saunters up, "Is your house unlocked?"

"Yeah, why?"

She holds up a jumbled mess of her macrame rope and says, "I'm going to decorate with these plant hangers like you said I could."

"Have at it, hot stuff."

"Okey-dokey, Quinn Maverick Evans." She says with a tiny glare.

I laugh, "That would be a badass middle name like I'm Tom Cruise or something. Sadly, I'm not that cool."

She rolls her eyes. "I know you aren't that cool. Just had to check if your parents thought you might be." She strolls away, her magical giggle floating through the air.

About half an hour later, Roni, toting a rather large framed photo of a longhorn, hustles up to me and says, "I'm going to hang this and a few other manly photos that I have in your living room. It's dreadfully dull in there."

"Absolutely not. I like my walls empty. My guitars and your macrame-that's it." I state flatly.

"But-"

"No, buts. I don't like it, I don't want it. I like my, what did you call it? Dreadfully dull? Yeah, I like my house dreadfully dull."

She squints her eyes and huffs, "Fine." I watch her walk towards my house, still holding the picture.

It takes about 15 minutes before I reach a point where I can walk away from the almost completed she-shed. Entering my house, I have to bite back a groan.

"Roni, what the fuck?" I ask, looking at that stupid ox on my far wall and an assortment of other black and white animals doing animal things by my guitar collection.

She grins, "See how nice everything looks? These prints are super understated but really bring the room together."

"The room was brought together by bricks and the sheetrock and all that shit. Not a picture." I say, walking over and taking that ox off of my wall. Handing it to Roni, I remove the rest of her photos and say, "Now, we can take these back to your house, or you can leave them here, and I will put them in your Stabbin' Cabin when I finish it. Your choice."

The glare she was sending me immediately disappears at the words 'stabbin' cabin' and Roni starts to laugh her amazing snort-laugh.

"Stabbin' Cabin! I love that so much! That's the name of the shed! My Stabbin' Cabin!"

Chapter 5
Stupid Grin

Roni

I wander around my house with a basket, collecting half-full teacups to take to the kitchen. I have been trying to break this habit since I moved into this house, but alas, I seem destined to live amongst scattered teacups.

My thoughts stray to Quinn, as they do more often than I'd like. He's lived next door for a couple of months now, and I really enjoy his presence. He is rapidly becoming one of my favorite people with his jovial personality and easygoing attitude. We have dinner together most nights and he is the perfect part-time husband. My yard has never looked better and keeping him fed and his house clean takes practically no extra time.

I glance at the clock on the wall and realize that if I start now, I can finish the project I am working on before I need to start dinner. I have been working remotely as a book editor for the last twenty years. It has been the perfect job for me. I love to read and have a knack for editing, and it has allowed me to travel all over the country.

After placing the cups in the sink, I go into my rarely-used office and start setting up my laptop on my thrift store desk. The room is pretty dull, as I usually work in the sunroom, but occasionally, it's nice to use an actual desk.

I really should decorate in here, especially since I now have Quinn to move stuff around and haul thrifted furniture for me. Speaking of Quinn, I have an overwhelming urge to yell a middle name at him, so I dance right out my door and head towards his house.

Quinn

We're watching the game when my front door flings open, as it often does when Roni comes over unannounced, and she yells "Quinn Zander Evans!" from the doorway.

"Wrong again, hot stuff!" I holler back as Kenny and I laugh.

"Gosh dang it! One day. One day." She says menacingly as she walks backward out the door.

I'm still grinning when Kenny turns to me with a serious expression, "Dude. You need to watch yourself."

"What are you talking about?"

"You and Roni. You have a stupid grin on your face and haven't stopped talking about that woman all afternoon."

"She lives right next door. We spend a lot of time together. Of course, I'm going to talk about her." I say, a sinking feeling in my gut.

"That sounds like a load of bullshit. I knew this was a bad idea. Roni is going to chew you up and spit you out."

"That doesn't even sound like Roni. Besides, it's just not like that."

"Do you know how long her longest relationship was?"

"Yep, she was seeing this chick for about a year altogether."

"Exactly. I haven't seen you this into a woman since Amanda, and we all know how big of a mistake that was."

I get frustrated and snap, "Roni is nothing like Amanda, and you know it."

"Yeah, Roni isn't out for your money. But you have to admit, neither woman is for you long term."

"Listen, what happens or doesn't happen between me and Roni isn't your business."

Kenny holds his hands up, "OK, OK, I'll stop. Just be careful."

"I never am."

"That's what worries me."

Me too, buddy, me too.

Chapter 6
I'm going to decapitate him.

Roni

"Stop! Holy fuck! What are you doing?" I scream as I jump out of my jeep and run toward Quinn, who is mowing down my sunflower seedlings! They were just sprouting and now they're probably all dead, decapitated by that motherfucker and his lawnmower.

I'm going to decapitate him.

He startles when he notices me and immediately turns the mower off.

"What's wrong? Are you okay?" His eyes are full of concern, but that does nothing to ease my panic.

"What's wrong?" I scream with tears flowing down my face. "You killed my sunflowers! They were just starting to grow! I've been wanting sunflowers for years and now they're dead!" I'm being irrational, I know, but I just can't help it. He looks so devastated that I immediately feel bad, but the anger is still coiled around my body like an anaconda squeezing me to death.

"I'm so so sorry-" He says, but I cut him off with a "No! Nothing for you to be sorry for. I didn't tell you they were there. You were being nice and cutting the grass. I'm just really upset. I can't be around you right now. I'm mad, but not at you, okay? I'll talk to you tomorrow." I say as I begin walking inside.

"Roni, can I go get you dinner or anything? I'm so sorry." Quinn asks from behind me.

"No. Thanks, just no. Tomorrow. I'll see you tomorrow."

"Okay. Tomorrow. Call me if you need anything."

I practically run into the house, not wanting Quinn to see me cry.

My sunflowers.

It's not a big deal.

They are just flowers.

I can plant more. I have planted more. I have all sorts of flowers in my garden.

I just can't stand it when someone changes my home. It makes my skin crawl and the anger builds until I just explode. I'll have to cook Quinn a really good dinner tomorrow to make up for it. I walk straight inside, barely holding it together-ish, and into my bathroom. Lights out, I sit on the toilet and sob. My flowers. My thoughts spiral out of control as I convince myself that Quinn hates me and that's why he destroyed my sunflowers. No one has ever loved me and they never will because I can't hold it together. They will all leave me if given the chance. Just like my parents. All I do is make things unpleasant. If I could just bend a little, maybe things would be different.

I grab my journal and write these toxic thoughts down; over and over, I hate myself until my sobs ease and the words cease.

I shove the journal into the drawer, taking deep breaths and letting my heart rate slow down.

Now that I can think again, I feel so bad about Quinn. I'm not quite ready to face him, so I'll make a cup of tea, read a little, and then go apologize.

After my tea has steeped and I add my honey, I grab the book I am currently reading, The Mistakes I Made, and become immersed quickly. Ginger, as if sensing I need comfort, curls herself up on my lap. I'm able to release some of the rage and hurt and replace it with the emotional time the characters are having when the doorbell rings, jolting me from the story so I sit my book and cat down and answer the door to see a very contrite-looking Quinn on my doorstep holding a bag from Waffle House and a bouquet of sunflowers.

My eyes burn as they fill with tears and I ask, "What are you doing?"

"Well, fuck, Roni. I felt like shit for mowing down your sunflowers. I know you were looking forward to them. So I figured I'd keep you in sunflowers until you can grow new ones and who doesn't want Waffle House for dinner when they feel like shit?"

I let out a watery laugh, this man is one of the good ones, for sure.

"Thank you, but this wasn't necessary. I'm not mad at you. I just can't stand my things getting changed without me doing it, you know? And I've never been able to have sunflowers before, even though they are my favorite flowers. I'm so sorry that I freaked out."

"No worries, I've known this about you practically since the day we met. Want to have dinner with me, or do you still need to be alone?"

"No, no. Come on in. Let's eat in the sunroom, yeah?"

"Yeah, babe."

I put the flowers in an oversized mason jar of water, place the whole thing on a stack of books in the sunroom, and then sit in the chair next to Quinn. He hands me a takeout container and a plastic spork and we both start eating. My emotions are all over the place. I know it wasn't his fault but I just can't help the hurt and rage I felt.

However, him bringing over sunflowers, Waffle House, and sitting with me in silence has gone a long way to brighten my mood.

I feel the tension slowly drain from my neck and shoulders the longer we sit and eat. In silence. Ginger weaves between our legs, further helping me calm down. Quinn keeps glancing at me as if to check on me and I know I should hate that, but it's...nice. Sweet even. Who knew this gruff construction worker was quite this sweet?

That thought sends a flutter of panic down my spine, and I jump up, breaking the mood.

"Want to watch a movie? I feel like lying around and not thinking."

"Sounds like a good time. I'm in."

"I need to jump in the shower if you don't mind. I need to wash the stress off of me. Then we can watch the movie."

"Of course, pretty lady. Need help washing between your little piggies?" He wiggles his eyebrows at me like a creep.

"Absolutely not, horrible man!" I say, laughing as I stick my tongue out at him and prance off into the bathroom to wash the panic of the day away. His deep laughter follows me and warms my heart.

Chapter 7
Soft Home Invasion

Quinn

While Roni showers I roam around her house, picking up half-full teacups and moving them to the sink, touching plants, looking at her collection of photos from her travels. Hot jealousy swirls through my veins as I look at picture after picture of her with other guys. I have no right to this jealousy; she isn't my girl. But the carefree joy in her eyes as she hugs these men does something to my insides, and I don't like it.

The front door suddenly bangs open, and a loud "Honey! I'm home!" rings out, and I spin around, coming face to face with big blue eyes and a blonde pixie cut. She lets out the cutest damn squeak and quickly glances around as if verifying her location.

"Hey, I'm Quinn. Do you know Roni?" God, I hope they do or else this is the softest home invasion ever.

"Quinn!" she says happily. "I've heard so much about you! I'm Valentine Mosby, call me Val. They/them pronouns, if you please.

Tell me you haven't killed my Ver-Ver and taken over her home, that'd be very uncool of you."

I let out a startled chuckle before saying, "Nothing that serious. She's in the shower."

"Cool, cool. Where is that beast of burden that she insists is just a sweet angel baby? I must greet her before I bring in my actual sweet angel baby." Knowing she had been summoned, Ginger makes her way through my legs and up to Val before rubbing against their legs. They crouch down, giving the cat snuggles, only to be rewarded with her teeth.

"God damn it! Every fucking time. One of these days, I swear..." Val trails off, rubbing the bite mark and glaring at the cat.

"Long-standing feud?" I ask with a smirk.

"Oh, yeah. This damn cat is my most reviled nemesis. But I brought my secret weapon. Give me a sec!" They cackle as they walk out the front door and skip out to the battered turquoise Subaru Forester that has shockingly pink rims and bumpers and...is the Subaru logo covered to say Su-bu-Wu with a UwU next to it? I bark out a laugh-it is! Val opens the one teal door and a grumpy-looking basset hound jumps out, howling the whole time. I chuckle and glance down at the cat as she hisses and runs into the bedroom. Once inside, Val says, "Quinn, I'd like you to meet Natalya. She is the superior animal, but don't agree with me. Ver-Ver hates that shit."

"Quinn, whatever you are listening to out there sounds just like my- VAL! WHAT ARE YOU DOING HERE!" Roni practically screeches the last sentence as she slides into the living room, almost colliding with a bookshelf and coffee table in her rush to hug her friend.

Val laughs and says, "Damn, a couple years in a cottage in the woods and you're already making strange witch sounds. The locals will be by soon with the pitchforks or something."

I can tell that I have quickly become the third wheel in this group and say, "Looks like you two have some catching up to do. I'll make myself scarce. I'm going to fix that shutter and finish mowing the lawn. Before I forget again, Roni, Ma asked me if you want to come over for dinner tomorrow. She's cooking, so it'll be really good."

"Oh! Yes! Will I get to meet your sisters, too?

"You will, though now I am not sure I want you to. Y'all are going to gang up on me aren't you?" I ask, concerned.

"I sure do hope so!" She says with glee.

Roni

I close the door behind Quinn, still giggling over his worried face, before turning to the platonic love of my life.

Val smirks at me before saying, "You didn't tell me he was hot."

"I'm sure that I mentioned he was attractive."

"Nope," They say, popping the p dramatically. "You said he was a little older, a construction worker, a cool guy, a great part-time husband, and loved your cooking. You said he had a nice sense of humor and was handy with tools. You said nothing about his perfect beard, sweet eyes, and that ass that someone should take a bite out of. Or the way his sleeves are just a smidge stretched by his thick arms. You definitely didn't say that he dressed like a blue-collar dreamboat. So that makes me wonder."

"There is nothing to wonder about. He's my friend. You're gorgeous, and I don't go running around telling everyone that. Jesus Christ on a cranberry cracker." I say with an eye roll. I know I sound defensive when Val starts laughing. Dang it.

"Yes, yes. You don't go running around waxing poetic about my beauty. But you have called me at three AM from a bar in Manhattan to tell me all about the gorgeous bartender who winked at you. You spent fifteen minutes describing his eye color. You want to screw your husband. And you can't because that would quite literally be shitting where you eat," they say with a giggle.

"It wouldn't be literally shitting where I eat," I say distractedly.

"Like I give a shit."

I laugh and wave my hand around as if to shoo away this conversation and ask, "So, how long are you in town for?"

"Forever, I think," Val says bashfully.

I grab their hand and drag them into the kitchen. I need a cup of tea, for sure. I get the kettle going and demand that they tell me everything. "But you were happy in Chicago, right?"

"For sure. But Memaw is considering selling the farm, and I want to help her. Besides, I missed you, and if you're settling down, I figured I could try it. Not like we can't pack up and go if it gets boring."

"That's the best part! We've been nomadic for so long that settling down feels like an adventure. Maybe we can find you a part-time husband, too!" I say, laughing.

"Maybe you can share Quinn with me. I wouldn't mind watching that ass bend over my sink."

A hot stab of jealousy hits me right in the gut. "Absolutely not. He's mine."

"Yours, huh?" Val says with a smug smile.

"Oh, fuck off. You know what I mean."

"Yup. You're going to screw the brains out of your part-time husband."

"I don't like this conversation anymore."

Chapter 8

Friends with benefits...fuck my life.

Quinn

"**I**s that her?" My sister's voice screeches from the kitchen; damn it, Roni hasn't even set foot in the house, and I'm ready to rescue her from my family. Roni's magical giggle rings from behind me and I relax. She is going to have a blast.

I hope. I'm having my doubts as my two younger sisters, just tiny blurs of brown hair and jeans, practically snatch her into the house and hustle her into the kitchen without even letting me do the introductions.

My two sisters, both spitting images of my mother, are petite and freckle-faced with deep chocolate brown hair and eyes. In recent years, silver has threaded through my momma's hair, though before that, she and my sisters were often mistaken for siblings.

My dad, whom I look just like, pulls me in for a hug with a chuckle. "I see we lost your woman before I even got to meet her."

"She's not my woman. Just a friend." I say with a smile.

"If you say so, then it must be so."

Well, hell. That's Pop's way of letting me know he doesn't believe me, but he acknowledges I believe it. But in this case, he is wrong.

"Damn it, you hussies! Bring me back my friend with benefits!" I holler.

Immediately after the collective feminine gasp from the kitchen and my father's booming laugh, I realized what I had said.

Within the hearing range of my mother.

The same mother that wanted me married and doing dad shit a decade ago.

Well, shit.

"What did he just say?" I hear my mother ask, and then I hear Roni's snort-laugh.

"It's an inside joke of sorts. Has he told you about my plea for a part-time husband? Yeah, he started referring to me as his friend with benefits because I cook and clean for him. Unfortunately, he calls me that literally everywhere. Like, who has them page their friend with benefits at the Piggly Wiggly? He didn't even need to! I had my damn phone!"

The laughter coming from the kitchen makes my heart do a little jump.

Better cut that shit out.

"It was funny!" I yell towards the kitchen, listening to my favorite women laugh.

Pop and I catch each other up on life and work, and my brother-in-law Donny joins in, just like we do every month when Ma decides she wants to cook.

Donny is about my size, as is my brother-in-law Chris. But no one would mistake us for real brothers, with Donny having blue eyes and blonde hair while Chris is all tan skin and black hair.

After a bit, I get the urge to lay eyes on Roni and make sure my sisters haven't scared her away.

"Come on, Pop." I say, "Let me introduce you to my ole' lady."

"I wouldn't say shit like that where your momma can hear it."

He chuckles as he follows behind me into the kitchen. I love my momma's kitchen. It's a kitchen made for cooking, with shelves of spices, flour, and sugar, and it always smells amazing. My mom went through a rooster phase in the 90s and never got over it, so everything is covered in those annoying birds. She even found rooster decals to put on the fridge and a set of chickens wearing human clothes to put over her sink. I swear Ma laughed for months over those pictures.

I'm grinning as I walk into the kitchen, and that turns into a full-blown smile when I find Roni huddled up with my sisters, heatedly debating which chocolate chip cookie recipe will yield the best cookies. All I can see is my sisters' dark hair mixing with Roni's wild blonde hair as they lean over the cookbook. My mom walks up to me with a smug smile, graying hair piled on her head, and says, "She fits right in with your sisters. Consider locking this one down."

I, a 43-year-old construction worker, roll my eyes.

And Pops smacks me upside the head with a grumble: "Don't you go rolling your eyes at your momma."

"Sorry, Ma. But Roni and I are just friends. She isn't looking to get married any more than I am."

My mom sighs, glances at Roni and my sisters, pulling ingredients for the cookies, giggling, and acting like they've been best friends their whole lives.

Roni looks up to see me grinning at her, so she rolls her eyes and turns back to my sisters.

"Have y'all seen Quinn's house yet?" Roni asks my sisters.

I groan, knowing she is fixing to start shit.

"We haven't. He keeps putting us off," Nicole says, throwing a glare my way.

Roni laughs; this is the first time her laughter has ever brought dread to my soul. She is going to sic my sisters on me as payback for not letting her decorate my house.

"It's bare. Nothing on the walls except his guitars, no rugs, just an ugly couch and snazzy recliner. His bedroom has a bare basic bed frame and an ancient nightstand. He won't let me do a damn thing in there, even though it desperately needs it."

Amber squeals and says, "Oh my god! I have that huge picture of the mountains in my attic. I could bring that."

"And I can bring over those framed photos I took down at the lake. They're just hanging in our spare bedroom since I didn't have anywhere else to hang them. They would look nice with that mountain picture." Nicole says excitedly.

"I made him some macrame plant hangers, but that's all he let me put up in his house," Roni interjects, smirking as I imagine my blank walled place looking like Roni's overflowing house.

"Look, y'all can bring a few things. Do a few things. But I don't like any clutter or nonsense in my house." I say, trying to let them know that I'm in charge of my own house, damn it!

They all look at me with sympathy and start laughing.

Fuck my life.

I make a quick exit from the kitchen, not waiting for them to decide to change more shit in my house. Donny claps me on the shoulder, laughing, "You might want to lock that one down; seeing as how she is running your life, you should at least be in her bed."

I sigh, looking at the ceiling. "Dear Lord, it's me again. Please save me from matchmaking mothers and brothers-in-law."

My sister Nicole's husband, Chris, walks up, "Finally got the kids settled," he says before glancing around. "What'd I miss?"

"Quinn's friend is already running his life, and he doesn't even have the benefit of sleeping with her."

"Alright, boys, let Quinn work at his own pace. If they're meant to be, it'll happen." Pops interrupts their joking, saving my ass.

We shoot the shit for the next hour, the laughter from the kitchen filling the house, now and then one of us would try to help in the kitchen only to be swatted away.

The cookie timer dings and the women folk yell for us to come eat, wonderful smells filling the dining room as we shuffle in. Roni, my sisters, and Ma are all giggling together at one end of the table, leaving us men at the other. I'm a little disappointed at not getting to sit near Roni. I got used to having meals being just us two. But damn, it was nice seeing her become best friends with my sisters. They haven't liked any woman I've dated, but it isn't surprising that they love Roni.

Dinner is a boisterous affair, with everyone yelling over the others and jokes and laughter. I can't stop staring at Roni, those cute little smile lines on the side of her mouth. The way her hair is never tame, waves and curls haphazardly thrown into a braid. She catches my eye and sticks out her tongue, making my sisters laugh. I wink at her and go back to my meal, thrilled that Roni and my family get on so well. Pops even offered her the last roll, which enlisted some gasps because he's damn greedy with Ma's rolls.

The ride back home was quiet, with contentment wrapped around us. And when we got home, Roni kissed my cheek, making my heart pound, before running inside.

Oh, I am in so much trouble.

Chapter 9
Boxers and a Grin

Roni

I fling open Quinn's door, even though I'm always a little afraid that a girl will be in there with him. That would be horrifying. The idea makes my chest feel a little tight, but there is no way in hell that I am examining that emotion. But he told me to just come on in and so I do.

Quinn is standing in the kitchen, wearing nothing but his boxers and a grin. "Well, hiya there, Sunflower. Come on in."

"Sunflower?" I ask with a giggle.

"Yup," he says, popping the p. If ever I feel dark and gray, I can just face you and let you be my sunshine."

My heart squeezes.

Ewe. Screw that. This is my part-time husband. Who cares if he is gorgeous? And thoughtful. And his deep red boxer briefs leave so little to the imagination. And he is so sweet.

Jesus Christ on a cranberry cracker.

"Okay, Romeo." I chuckle. Are you going to put pants on? Or is today underwear day?"

"Excuse me, dearest wife of the part-time variety, but you came over to my house on the weekend. I'm not getting dressed again until Monday. And since today is Sunday, boxers it is!"

I snort-laugh and say, "Well, okay, then."

"What brings you to my neck of the woods, Sunflower?"

"Oh! Yes! Can I watch a movie on your snazzy big TV?"

"Oh, sure. Go ahead. I was just puttering around here. What are you watching?"

"The Last Holiday with Queen Latifah? It's my favorite, and it occurred to me that I haven't watched it on an actual TV, ever, I don't think. And once I thought that I couldn't stop thinking about it and how lucky I am that my husband of the part-time variety has a big ole tv."

"Lucky, indeed. I haven't seen this one. What's it about?"

"Oh, my goodness! Seriously? It's just about the best romantic comedy ever! So, Queen Latifah is this meek, shy woman who really isn't living, just going through the motions. And then there is LL Cool J just scowling around until he sees Georgia - That's Queen Latifah's character - and that's the only time he smiles, is looking at her! Isn't that just the sweetest? Anyway. She gets told that she only has a few weeks left to live, and she cashes out her 401k and all of those other grown-up retirement money deals and flies over to Europe. She stays in a super fancy hotel, eats good food, and charms the pants off of everyone. Then LL Cool J finds her, and the doctor tells her it was a mistake, and they open a restaurant. Happily Ever After! Doesn't it sound wonderful?"

Quinn laughs and says, "Sure, want some company?"

"Yes! Absolutely! I brought snacks!"

"Talking my language, woman. Whatcha got?"

"I brought popcorn and sour gummy bears!"

Quinn looks disappointed, "That's it?"

"I was going to watch a movie. What else should I have brought?"

"I don't know. I was hoping that you made a pie or maybe some of those cookies you made last week. Or those Martha Washington balls. Those are what my dreams are made of, dear."

"Okay, okay." I say to his sad puppy eyes, "I'll go see what I have in the freezer."

Quinn prowls behind me on the way to my house and freezer. "Do you just want to look?" I ask him, stepping to the side.

"God, yes. Move, woman." He growls as he digs through my huge, deep freeze.

"Hell yeah!" He exclaims, pulling out a small bag of Martha Washington balls and another of peanut butter balls. He happily grumbles to himself as he pulls out a bag of cookies.

"This should do it!"

"You want some sweet tea to go with?" I ask with a smile, already knowing the answer. He can only nod since he has already started on the candy.

"Cool, cool. You go on, I'll grab the tea and head over." All I get in return is a closed-mouth smirk and a thumbs-up because his mouth is now full of frozen cookies.

That man, I swear.

Quinn

We settle in my living room, me in the recliner and Roni stretched out on my couch. She put the frozen cookies in the oven for a few minutes to warm them up, I told her that it was fine. They taste great frozen, but she insisted. And damn if she wasn't right. Warm and gooey, her chocolate chip cookies are some of the best that I've ever had.

Don't tell my Ma, though.

I glance over to ensure she is comfortable before pressing play on this chick flick. I'm not particularly interested, but if it makes Roni happy, I'm in.

She suddenly sits up and says, "Maybe we ought not to watch this today."

Concerned, I ask, "Why not?"

"Because there is a lot of food in it, like really good food, and I haven't cooked today. You are going to be so hungry by the end." She laughs.

"I've got cookies and candy, I think I'll survive," I chuckle, pressing play.

"Alright, don't grumble to me about how hungry you are."

I laugh as the opening credits go by.

Less than five minutes into the movie, my stomach is growling, causing Roni to laugh and throw a gummy bear at me. I pop it into my mouth and mumble, "That chicken just looked really good. And I love sausage. Do you have any Conecuh?"

Roni sits cross-legged on the sofa, laughing. "I told you that we should have waited! I could have cooked us something, and we could have eaten in here. But no, you didn't want to listen to me."

"Well, I'm listening now."

She dramatically lays back, hand on her forehead like a swooning southern belle, and says, "You're going to work me to death, Quinn Lawrence Evans."

I bark out a laugh, "Wrong again, Sunflower!"

"One day I'm going to guess right, you dreadful man. You want Conecuh, rice, and some tomato slices?"

Guilt starts to seep in, covering my hunger. I don't want to actually put her to work when all she wanted was to watch a movie.

"Nah, sweet young thang, you don't have to cook for me. I'll be alright. I'm just picking at you."

"You goober, I really don't mind. I didn't have lunch so sausage sounds good. Come keep me company while I cook, and then we'll bring it over here and sit in front of the TV and eat." She says, tossing one last gummy bear in her mouth as she stands.

"If you're sure, Conecuh and rice sounds real good."

Excited, I follow her out the door and to her house, greeting Ginger at the door. I'm not really a cat fellow, but this one is pretty cool. Sweet, affectionate but still independent enough to do her own thing most of the time. Kind of like Roni, actually. I give her scratches behind her ears and am rewarded with her nuzzling my hand. The Siamese meanders into the kitchen, weaving around Roni's gorgeous legs as Roni reaches down to pet her.

After Ginger has had enough of us, we wash our hands, and Roni starts gathering ingredients to cook for us. I'm tasked with rinsing the rice while she whirls around the kitchen, chopping and frying the sausage, chatting and laughing. It's like a dance, her in the kitchen, and I can't stop watching her, enthralled.

She stops in front of me with a smirk and takes the rice from my hand. Her scent of sunscreen and vanilla halts my brain activity. How did I never notice just how good she smells? I want to burrow into her neck and inhale.

Shit. No. This is my friend, my buddy Roni.

The woman that keeps me fed.

Laughing to myself, I push away from the sink and sit at Roni's scarred kitchen table. Roni would kill me if she thought I was lusting after her.

"What's so funny, big guy?" Roni asks, her head tilted to the side.

"Just thinking about how it took less than ten minutes into that movie before you were proven right," I lie, shaking my head.

Roni giggles that magical giggle, "I knew that as soon as she started cooking, it would be all over."

She grabs a tomato from the fridge and starts slicing it onto our plates, before adding a generous serving of rice and sausage.

I stand up and take the plates from her, "Are we heading back to my house?"

"Yep, but hand me the plates and go grab a couple of my floor pillows and some of the blankets out of the basket, will you?" She asks, reaching out for the food.

I reluctantly hand her the food, not wanting to relinquish control of the delicious grub and snag the items she requested.

Roni

I carry our plates across the yard while Quinn carries a couple of my floor pillows and blankets.

"What are we doing with all the pillows and blankets? You aren't trying to add more decorations to my house are you?" Quinn asks as he opens his door.

"Of course not. Those are my favorite floor pillows. Just toss them on the floor." I say, laughing at his disgruntled expression.

I sit our early dinner on his kitchen table and go set up the pillows in front of his coffee table and throw the blankets over them.

"There, it's almost a nest. We can sit on the pillows, leaning against the sofa, and eat off the coffee table," I say while he grimaces.

"Sounds like I won't be able to get my big ass off the floor." He grumps.

"You can sit on the couch, it's your house. I just thought it would be fun." I say, grabbing our dinner off the table, bringing it over to the coffee table, and making myself comfortable on the pillow and blanket mound. Quinn looks down at me chuckling before plopping down right next to me. Shoulder to shoulder we start the movie. Quinn shovels food into his mouth, patting my thigh in appreciation, as we watch the movie.

Soon enough, our plates are empty and Quinn is rubbing his stomach.

"Woman, that was delicious," He sighs happily and wraps an arm around my shoulders to pull me in for a squeeze.

"Now, where are the rest of the snacks? I could really go for some popcorn," he says pulling his arm from around me and grabbing our plates to take to the sink. I start laughing when he rummages in my bag of snacks, pulling bowls and pouring gummy bears, popcorn, and the goodies from my freezer into them. I hop up to help him carry them to the table and he grabs my arm, pulling me in for a hug. My heart skips a beat, which is pretty damn inconvenient. I kiss his cheek and pull away, flustered.

"Hey, you okay?" He asks as I start grabbing bowls.

"Of course," I smile up at him, "We just forgot to pause the movie and I don't want to miss it."

"It's fine, we can just rewind it a bit."

"Right, I always forget about that," I chuckle, feeling a little awkward.

We set up the snacks on the coffee table and get cozy on the floor pillows again. This time Quinn tosses his arm over my shoulder and tucks me into his side. I'm so aware of being pressed against Quinn's body that I can barely focus on the movie.

He nudges me, "She isn't really going to die, is she?"
I laugh, the tension broken, "You'll just have to keep watching."

"She isn't going to die," He says, uncertain.

I giggle, pat him on the chest, and lay my head on him. He sighs and squeezes me just a little bit tighter.

Chapter 10

A spider stole the teacups.

Quinn

I'm trying to focus on playing the guitar, strumming along to a rock song, and thinking about how good Roni felt snuggled against me last weekend. It's been a good handful of months since I moved in here, and I thank my lucky stars every day that I did. Sunflower is amazing, a great cook, and so fun to be around. Sure, I'm attracted to her, but I'll never do anything to jeopardize this good thing I've got going.

I finally zone out only to be interrupted by Roni screeching "Quinn!" and in the next second, my front door slams open, and with it, my stomach just drops right out of my ass. Roni is jumping around, tattoos on display, wearing these tiny black boy-short panties, her dimpled cheeks peeking out from the bottom, and a nearly see-through tank top. And no bra. No fucking bra.

Oh, my god. She is yelling at me.

Oh, fuck.

I open my mouth to apologize for noticing her hard nipples.

Oh fuck, focus.

Luckily, before I can spit out the apology, her screeches become English in my brain. A spider in her bathroom nearly killed her and stole the teacups, it seems.

"Are you even listening to me?" She yells, clearly frustrated with my vivid mental life; but fuck, what does she expect with that little curve of her stomach poking out of the bottom of her tank top?

She is going to murder me. Focus.

"Of course, I'm listening. You need me to kill a spider in the bathroom. I'm on it."

"No! Absolutely not! You aren't killing the spider, you will catch and release him. But also, the spider is not in my bathroom. He is in the kitchen, over the teacups. And I have a moth in the bathroom that I would also like for you to remove." Shit, I was super incorrect there.

I open my hall closet and slide my feet into a pair of hot pink crocs to follow her over to her place. Hopefully, she'll focus on the Crocs and forget to be mad at me about the not-listening deal.

"QUINN! THEY'RE PINK!" she yells and then the magical giggle just tinkles out.

"Yeah, yeah. Someone told me that a neon pair of Crocs are the best house shoes and here we are."

"Oh! They absolutely are! That someone must be rather brilliant."

"She definitely is."

As we walk into her house, all I can think about is if she is going to change into clothes that don't show every gorgeous flower tattoo trailing down her legs and those sexy blue veins behind her knees. I bite my knuckle to keep from groaning. Fuck, she is hot.

I can't catch and release her critters with her looking like this.

Luckily, she merely gestures to the kitchen and says that she will not return until it is spider-free and goes into her bedroom. Right after Mr. Spider is transferred to a nearby tree, she emerges wearing a pair of holey, baggy jeans, a floral lace tank top, and Docs. And the swooping of my traitorous stomach proves that Sunflower is smoking hot regardless of her attire.

"Did you get him?" She asks, squinting at the corner where the spider once lived.

"Of course I did, it's in my job description," I chuckle.

She giggles that magical sound, and says, "Thank you. I'm not really terrified of them, but they give me the heebie-jeebies so bad."

"Sure sounded like you were terrified of them, but that's okay. You now have a big and strong part-time husband to be your full-time critter catcher," I say, flexing my muscles and laughing.

"My hero," Roni says, imitating Olive Oil.

She then glances at the clock on the wall and says, "Do you want to hang out while I cook? I'm just making some pork chops and rice. Maybe some black-eyed peas. Won't take too long."

"Absolutely; want to put me to work?"

"Sure, measure up and rinse the rice for me, please."

"On it. After we eat, do you want to go for a ride on my bike? I feel like watching the sunset at the pier." I cross my fingers, hoping she says yes. A nice easy ride on a beautiful day with this woman wrapped around me sounds like heaven.

"Ooooh! It's been ages since I've ridden on a motorcycle! Yes, please! Instead of cooking, I could make us some sandwiches and we could have a picnic! How about that?"

"Sounds good, babe. You going to make me stop by that coffee shop that you and Val are always going on about?"

"Obviously," she says, rolling her eyes.

Good. She is really going to enjoy my most recent bike addition.

"Alright, then. I'll go get dressed to go, you can fix up the grub. And you need sleeves, please. Or you can just wear my leather jacket since it'll be warm enough for your tank top at the beach."

"I'll wear your leather jacket and pretend that I'm in one of those motorcycle club books. We can be fleeing the scene." She says, laughing.

Roni

Quinn tosses me his leather jacket and straddles his bike. The soft denim stretches across his thick thighs, and I—well, I need to stop staring at my friend like this. I shove my arms into the oversized jacket and sling my leg behind Quinn, enjoying being pressed against him.

Too soon we arrive at the coffee shop and park in the back.

"Am I going to hit my head on a hanging basket in here, too?" Quinn asks, looking amused.

"Where did you hit your head on a basket?" I ask, confused.

"That tea place. I couldn't turn around in there without bumping into something."

I laugh as we walk inside, gesturing to the sofas, tie-dye curtains, and enough room for a massive man like Quinn to turn around.

"Does this meet your standards?" I smirk.

"It'll do. Okay, Sugar Pie, I'm not a coffee shop guy. So get me whatever you get, as long as it's as sweet as you."

I crack up, "So extremely bitter and rather unpleasant?"

He nudges my side, staring up at the brightly colored menu board, "Hush your mouth and order me something tasty."

"I already planned on making you try my favorite drink. Val and I don't even look at the menu anymore." I giggle.

I order our frozen mocha coffees, and before I can pay, Quinn snatches my debit card and inserts his instead. I just roll my eyes and hand the barista my punch card. One day, I will actually keep up with one, fill it, and get a free coffee.

One day.

Our drinks are made quickly so we grab them and walk back to the bike.

"Shit, can we even carry drinks on your motorcycle? Maybe if you go really really slow?" I ask, hoping for a solution.

"Didn't I mention that I got you a present?" Quinn says with a grin as he flips open one of his saddlebags to reveal a snazzy cup holder.

I squeal, "You did not get these just for me!"

"Of course, I did. Ordered them a few weeks ago."

"But why?" I ask.

"Because you keep talking about loving this coffee place. I figured it was only a matter of time before we ended up here." He chuckles.

I jump into his arms for a big hug and kiss his cheek.

"You really are the sweetest man to ever exist," I say.

He just rolls his eyes and shoves his head into his helmet.

I'm left feeling tingly and very aware of this man as I slide in behind him and we take off.

Quinn

Holy fuck. My entire body feels hot and I'm sure that I have sweat my deodorant off. Roni felt way too good in my arms, gotta squash that shit. Getting all hot and bothered about the lady that feeds me is just asking for trouble. Besides all that, I really like Roni. I want to keep her in my life and a fling will certainly ruin all of that.

But who says it has to be a fling?

Shut up.

It's about an hour until sunset and we manage to snag a table on the grassy side of the pier. Roni unpacks the picnic while I try to keep from snatching the food from her. Her magical giggle rings out as she sits a paper plate in front of me loaded up with a thick ham sandwich, a huge serving of fruit salad, and a tiny bag of chips.

Damn, guess she noticed that I was starving.

"You can not always be this hungry." She says.

"Oh, yes, I can. Especially for your food, woman." I reply, barely swallowing my food before talking, "I don't know what you did but this is the best damn sandwich I've ever had. Don't tell my momma."

"Ooh, I am so telling on you."

"Traitor."

Chapter 11
Kind of a bitch.

Roni

My bedside clock reads six AM as my phone ringing wakes me up. What the actual fuck? I see it's Val and quickly answer, "What's wrong?"

"Nothing's wrong, Nervous Nancy. I want to go to the beach today. Early. Like, we leave in an hour early. I'll meet you at your house and we'll take your jeep."

Still drowsy, I reply, "Are you 83? Going to the beach this early and calling me Nervous Nancy? Jesus. But fine, that actually works out perfectly. Ginger has a vet visit at 4, so as long as we leave by 2, I'll make it on time. Want me to pack a lunch or walk to the Waffle House?"

I can hear them rolling their eyes as they say, "Waffle House, obviously. So bring a hoodie."

"Duh."

We hang up and I hunt for my bikini and all the other beach things we might need. I just know Val is going to show up carrying a hoodie and wearing a bikini, and that's it. If I don't bring it, we won't have it.

I was just finishing up applying my sunscreen and brushing my teeth when I hear Val open my front door to yell, "Come on, Ver-ver, let's get this show on the road!"

I roll my eyes and walk into my living room to see that I was right; there Val stands, blonde shaggy pixie cut in disarray, wearing an oversized t-shirt with the sleeves cut off and a neon green bikini under it, clutching a pale pink hoodie.

"What's in the bag, hag?"

"All the shit you forgot, butt-face."

"I can not believe you called me a butt-face," Val says with a glare.

"It's early. I'll be creative later."

"Fair enough. Let's get this shit show started."

Val grabs my bag like the gentleman they are and off we go.

The beach is already crowded when we arrive, but it'll be much worse by lunchtime. We're able to snag a great spot, close enough to the water to play and still see our towels. Val immediately dumps my bag in the sand and takes off for the water. I quickly catch up and grab their arm.

"You need sunscreen."

"Ewe, no, Mom."

"Shut up, I'm not rubbing aloe on your back, so come here. I brought the spray kind. Close your eyes and hold your breath."

I spray them down, and off they run. It's been our habit since high school. Val runs into the water while I set up our area. The sunscreen is more recent, as teens all we were trying to do was get a tan. Right as I settle myself onto my towel and pull out a paperback romance novel, Val comes running up, dripping all over my book, digging in the cooler for a soda. So I reach around and push them over.

"Hey!" Val says, trying to get the sand off of their hands and ass.

"You were dripping on my book," I say with a shrug.

They shake their short blonde hair like a puppy, getting salt water all over me, my book, and everything else.

"I don't even know why I'm friends with you."

"Because you're kind of a bitch and most folks don't like that," Val says, laughing.

"Yeah, that checks out."

After laying in the sand and playing in the water, it was time to pack it up and walk over to the Waffle House. We deposit our items in the truck and cross the street, the freezing air conditioner blasting us in the face as we open the door. Instead of shivering, we decide to get our burgers to-go. We head back to my Jeep and climb in, windows down, the ocean breeze twisting our hair, and eat our greasy fare. Feeling lethargic, we snag an umbrella and the rest of our things and head back out to the sand. Finding a spot, we snooze and read and chat the rest of the day away, losing track of time.

We are both a little sunburnt, but this was a much-needed day. It's like the sun and beach super duper extra recharge my batteries.

As I pull out of the parking lot and onto the road that will take me straight home, traffic is at a standstill.

"Wonder what happened. Probably an accident or something. Could you check?" I ask Val as they are already pulling their phone out of the glove box.

"Yup, an accident. Looks like traffic will be at a standstill until they get it cleaned up."

"Oh my God," I say, panicking, "We were already late leaving, and now I am definitely not getting home in time to take Ginger to the vet. Damn it, will you call them and let them know?"

"Why don't we just ask Quinn? Doesn't he usually get home around 3 on Fridays?"

"Oh, yes. Yes. Will you text him?" I ask, mentally patting myself on the back for getting a part-time husband.

Quinn

This can't be that bad. I just have to grab the cat and get her to the vet. I make the 'pussy come here' sounds and search under the furniture in Roni's sunroom. I see Ginger peeking out from under a table and snag her. As if she knows what's up, she reaches around and claws the shit out of my arm.

"Fuck!" I roar-glaring at the little asshole as a drop of blood runs down my arm. She then manages to scratch my chest, claw snagging on my shirt, and then she runs off for parts unknown.

"Jesus Christ, cat. Where are you?" I bellow, really regretting every choice that has brought my life to this point.

I head towards the bedroom, expecting to find Ginger on the bed. I fluff the pillows around hoping she had burrowed into her favorite place, but no such luck.

A sense of dread tingles down my spine seconds before I hear a hiss and feel her razor-sharp teeth dig into my calf and her claws wrap around my leg. I fling my leg out, trying to dislodge her, but all I do is fall on my ass.

"GOD FUCKING DAMN IT."

Out of the corner of my eye, I catch her trying to sneak back up on me. I reach out quickly, grabbing her by the scruff of her neck, and lug her back into the sunroom where the carrier was left. I shove her in the carrier while she snarls and yells what I imagine are obscenities at me. Before I can get the damn thing zipped up, her murder mit strikes out, catching my wrist and scratching down onto my hand. I shove her back in and finally get it zipped up, both Ginger and I snarling and hissing at the indignities we have been exposed to.

Well, at least the hardest part is done.

I bandage my arm, wrist, and chest, rub my bruised ass and away we go.

Roni better be prepared to cook all of my demands for at least a week for this bullshit.

The ladies at the front desk all giggle and smile at me as I walk in, hair standing straight up, with a chonky, pissed-off siamese in a backpack looking like an astronaut until they check the computer for her appointment. Their smiles become forced as they tell me to have a seat, the vet will be right with us. Already frustrated, I ask them what could be so bad and they answer, "There are notes in her chart warning others about how mean she is. She is the only cat that has this sort of note in her chart." I laugh without humor, knowing they are right. That darn cat.

I sit down and look at Ginger. She glares at me and a sense of foreboding settles deep in my soul.

I am so screwed.

A few minutes later, a nice girl comes and takes Ginger to the back for bloodwork and all that jazz while I send out a few work emails from my phone. The door opens and I glance up, dread tingling down my spine when I see my ex-wife walk in with a tiny chihuahua. She glances over at me as she walks to the check-in counter and smirks. After checking in, but before I faked a work call that would take me outside and away from her, she saunters over and sits right next to me.

"Well, hello there. Been a while."

"Not long enough," I say with a sigh. This long day just became unbearably long.

She chuckles and rests her hand on my arm. "Always so sour. I'm just being friendly. You have a pet now?"

I remove her hand from my arm and reply, "I don't. I'm doing a favor for a friend."

"Must be a good friend," she says, batting her eyelashes at me.

"Don't you have a husband?" I snap, tired of her flirting.

"Not really, we've separated. Why? Interested?"

Luckily, before I lose my cool, the receptionist calls Amanda back.

I hear a commotion, and then the girl who took Ginger comes running out of the back, crying. She goes outside, lights a cigarette, and inhales it in practically one puff.

Oh, fuck.

A pinched-faced woman comes from the back. "Mr. Corbin?" she asks, looking at me. I realize with a start that she thinks I'm Roni's husband. My chest tightens at the thought, but that's just panic. Obviously.

"I'm Quinn Evans, Roni's friend." I correct her as I shake her hand.

She says that she had to subdue Ginger just to finish her checkup and that she should wake up and be fine in a couple of hours. I asked her if I could get a couple more doses to let Satan sleep longer, but she didn't find me funny. I decided not to shove the sleeping cat into her carrier since it's easier to tote the cat around in my arms like a baby.

Yes, I am a moron.

I pull up the drive just as Ginger wakes up two hours earlier than expected and she is pissed. She glares and vibrates with rage as I put my truck in park and slowly reach toward her, hoping she's dazed enough for me to snag and toss her into Roni's house. The spawn of Satan uses this moment to latch onto me and sink those rapier sharp teeth into my hand.

"FUCK," I roar, shaking my arm. She lets go and I jump out of the truck and shut the door, Ginger glaring at me from inside.

Shit, shit, shit. Just as I decide to go ahead and sign the truck over to Ginger and go buy myself a new one, Roni's Jeep comes rushing up the driveway- 90s gangster rap blaring from the speakers. She hops out, all sun-kissed and wild-haired, barefoot and beautiful. She looks like summer and I all but forget about the cat as I watch her walk towards me.

"Oh, my god! You're bleeding? What happened?" And just like that, I'm knocked from my stupor and remember that I'm pissed. "Your cat," I growl, pointing at my truck's window. I hear Val cracking up and I whip around to scowl at them, but I catch a glimpse of Roni trying not to laugh, her eyes all sparkling, and I can't help but chuckle.

"Jesus, woman. Your cat is a damn demon. You owe me." I say gruffly before tossing her my keys and stomping to my house.

Maybe I can't summon up any anger for that woman, but I can sure pretend to.

Then she calls my name and runs up to me, giving me a big hug and whispering in my ear that she'll cook my favorite dinners all week, with dessert, and I know I can't even pretend to be angry.

Roni

I pull the grill out, having decided to make Quinn steak, corn, and potatoes after the supposed trauma Ginger caused him. The food is almost done when Quinn comes sniffing around the corner.

"Whatcha cookin' good lookin'? And is some of it for me? I am starving after the ordeal I went through today."

"Steak, potatoes, corn on the cob. And, of course, some of it is for you. I promised your favorites for taking Ginger. Have you recovered enough to tell me how it went?"

"Well, she got her shots."

"Of course, she did. What had you so frazzled, though?"

"Your cat is Satan; that's what had me so frazzled."

I snort-laugh, especially once Quinn joins me. The laughter continues as Quinn tells me of his perilous time with my favorite feline. I finish grilling while he finishes his story, which must be full of untruths. My sweet angel baby would never do all of that. Sure, she enjoys terrorizing the vet techs, but who doesn't? When I say as much, jokingly, of course, Quinn unbuckles his belt.

"Whoa, Quinn Xavier Evans! What on earth are you doing?"

"I'm fixing to show you the bruise on my ass since you think your cat is so sweet."

I'm doing my best not to laugh, but it isn't working.

"Stop! I believe you!" I squeal, covering my eyes.

"Oh, no, you are going to see this. I earned that steak." He says, pulling down the left side of his pants and boxers, a nice view of part of his ass cheek and the beginnings of a huge bruise on his hip and top of his butt cheek.

"That proves nothing!" I say, trying to forget how nice his ass is.

"I fell trying to wrangle your damn cat!"

"Or you fell because you are clumsy, or you tripped! Couldn't be my sweet baby angel's fault." I say as I plate up Quinn's food and hand him the plate.

He sits in a lawn chair and shoves a piece of steak in his mouth, mumbling around it about how I better be glad that I'm such a good cook.

"What was that?" I ask, eyebrow raised.

He stutters like a deer in headlights, "Nothing, just, I, oh! I'm going out with Kenny tomorrow, so you won't need to cook me dinner."

"I'm sure that's what you said."

"It was!" He says, around a mouthful of steak.

Chapter 12

When she sings it's...atrocious.

Quinn

The bar is a bit more crowded than usual for a Wednesday night, but that's probably for the best since Kenny won't be able to interrogate me about Roni if we can't hear ourselves think. Not like there is anything to talk about, anyway. She's just my friend. My amazing, gorgeous friend. Just my friend. I park my ass at the bar to wait on Kenny and order our beers. When I see him heading my way, I'm surprised to see Rhonda with him. She's never come to hang out with us before. His wife is amazingly gorgeous, like a 90s supermodel, tall and curvy, with ebony skin and a shaved head. I always wonder how a short, thin, pale fellow like Kenny pulled her, but it is so obvious that they adore each other. He drops her off at a table full of women and heads my way. We do that man-hug thing and pop open our beers.

"Sorry, I made you wait. Rhonda set up a last-minute girls' night since I was already going to be here, then we had to drop the baby off at her momma's house. That took fucking forever. But they look like they're going to have a real good time if those shots are any sign," he says, gesturing towards his wife and the gaggle of broads yelling "woohoo" before downing a hot pink shot. I chuckle and then startle as I see Roni, wearing skin-tight jeans, combat boots, and a black tank top, saunter her way toward us.

"Well, hello there, husband. Buy me a Coke and Crown, will you? That fruity shit gives me heartburn." Roni asks as she kisses my cheek and pats Kenny on the arm.

"Sure thing, babes. I'll send it your way when the bartender gets to me. You gonna be a woo-girl tonight? Get a little wild?" I ask, wagging my eyebrows like a creep. Her magical giggle fills the space, drowning out all the other noise, and she says, "If you catch me woo-ing or hoo-ing tonight or any night, please do the humane thing and put a bullet in my brain. Okay? Okay. Good talk. Don't forget my Crown and Coke." The last sentence is thrown over her shoulder as she makes her way back to the girls, two gays, and Val.

Somehow, Kenny and I end up at the table with everyone else, and we haven't stopped laughing since sitting down. Watching a girl's night progress from the inside is a wild ride. Roni and Val are directly across from Kenny and me, sharing a chair and a drink, giggling and whispering. I find myself unable to look away and wonder if the 3 beers had way more alcohol than usual. There is no other way to explain how fascinating every single laugh line on Roni's face is. A commotion next to Kenny forces my eyes away from Roni and over to Rhonda and a couple of other ladies as they stumble over to the DJ. He laughs as Roni and Val boo. He announces they'll start the karaoke machine if anyone wants to sign up. The whole table of ladies rushes to the DJ booth and seemingly every other woman in the bar. Except for my Roni and Val, of course. They are rolling their eyes and scowling at the rest of the group. Then she raises her glass-Is that straight whiskey?-and gives me a smirk. My heart races as I grin and lose myself in her eyes before the singing on the stage pulls my focus. Damn, Rhonda is the dullest karaoke singer I've ever seen. She's decent enough to not be bad but not good enough to be entertaining. Once Rhonda has wrapped up her song, she points to Roni and starts getting the crowd worked up to encourage her to the stage. I watch as Roni shakes her head a couple times, rolls her eyes, reaches over the table, and snags Kenny's shot before pounding it down. She makes her way towards the stage, still shaking her head. She leans over the booth and flips through the binder of songs before laughing and pointing to one. The DJ is grinning as he gets it queued up. The opening strains of Bitch by Meredith Brooks play, and laughter fills the small dive bar. When she sings, it's...atrocious, to say the least. The woman couldn't find the tune if someone handed it to her, but damn, does she put on a show. An exceptional show, really. I can barely tear my eyes from her to glance around the room; she enraptures everyone. What she lacks in singing ability, she more than makes up for in stage presence and charisma.

Goddamn, my girl is amazing.

My girl?

Fuck.

No. Absolutely not.

My friend. My best friend, even. Not...my girl.

I look into her eyes as she sings a line about someone needing to be a stronger man, and one word wraps around my heart, squeezing all the breath from my lungs.

Mine.

Fuck.

Chapter 13
Vikings don't wear shirts.

Quinn

"Quinn Rocky Evans!" Roni yells as she flings my front door open. My heart jumps at the sight of her. I need to get a handle on that shit.

"Wrong again, Madame," I say with a chuckle.

"Ooh, Madame. Sounds like I run a whorehouse in 1873 California, I dig it. Anyways. Want to go to the Renaissance Faire with me next weekend? Val has a booth set up, but I want a friend to walk around and talk shit with."

Friend. I'm her friend. That's all she sees me as. I rub at the ache in my chest as I say, "Of course I'll go. I'm not dressing up, though."

"Oh, yes, you are!" she says, pouting her perfect lips.

How can I say no to that face?

"Fine! I'm not wearing tights, though!"

"Perfect! I'll handle our costumes, ok?"

"I'm terrified," I say with a fake shudder.

Roni snort-laughs and says, "You probably should be."

Oh, I am.

Over the next week, I witness multiple delivery drivers drop off packages at Roni's house. The way she glances at me and giggles makes me nervous about how she will be dressing me this weekend. Every evening over dinner, I beg her to tell me how I'll be dressed.

Roni just laughs and says, "You'll find out on Saturday. Well, Friday after work, because I need you to try everything on so I can fix whatever needs fixing."

"You better be glad that you cook so damn good, woman," I say, knowing that even if she didn't feed me, I'd still be following her around like a puppy.

Roni

Giggling to myself, I gather Quinn's full costume, walk barefoot across our yards, and fling open his door, "Quinn Jerome Evans, time to play dress-up!"

"Wrong again, Sunflower!" Quinn yells from the direction of his bedroom before walking into the living room. Shirtless and with wet hair, my mouth goes dry.

"Roni?" Quinn asks, with a bewildered look, "You ok?"

Realizing that I'm staring, I mentally shake myself out of it. Fuck, he's hot.

Stop it.

Friend. Friend. Friend.

I shove the clothes into his hands. "I'm fine. Sorry, zoned out there for a minute. Go try these on and come out so I can see."

He tilts his head to the side with a small smile. "Will do."

Damn it. He is only going to be hotter in his Viking getup. I breathe in and out slowly, trying to calm my racing heart, and sit on his sofa. His TV is on some home improvement show, so I try to focus on that instead of my ridiculous attraction to Quinn. No good can come from this.

He walks out of his bedroom in leather pants, with faux fur around his shoulders and a disgruntled expression.

Fuck.

"Where's the shirt, Roni?" He asks, scowling at me. It's cute.

I smile and say, "No shirt; Vikings didn't wear shirts."

"I'm sure a Viking somewhere wore a shirt at some point."

"Not at the Ren Faire!" I say, giggling, watching his face soften.

"Seriously, can I have a shirt?"

"Nope," I say, popping the p.

"Fine. Can I see what you are wearing?"

"Nope. It's a surprise."

"Your surprises kind of suck, Sunflower. Exhibit A," He says, gesturing to his shirtless chest.

"Fine. Do you really want me to tell you? I promise you won't look ridiculous next to me or anything."

"I don't want you to tell me. I want you to show me. Please? I'm begging you."

I roll my eyes and stomp out of his house, flinging, "Fine. I'll be back in a minute." over my shoulder.

I should be more concerned that I can't say no to this man. Instead, a bubbling sensation takes up residence in my chest.

Damn it.

Making my way into my bedroom, I pull the leather pants off of my clean clothes chair and have them halfway on when I realize the entire effect will be ruined if I show him now. I can't do the makeup and the faux-hawk. That'll take too long. I yank the leather pants off and march back to Quinn's house.

I fling his door open, shouting, "Quinn Eleanor Evans! I can't show you my outfit until tomorrow when I have the hair and makeup done!"

He laughs, "Eleanor? Isn't that a girl's name?"

"It's just what you deserve, distracting me like that."

"Distracting? How?"

Shit.

"Oh, never you mind," I say, scowling. "You'll have to wait until tomorrow to see my outfit, and that's that."

Baffled but smiling, Quinn says, "Just promise me I won't look ridiculous."

"Are you trying to hurt my feelings? You should know that I wouldn't do that to you. My outfit suits yours perfectly, and we will fit right in at the Ren Faire. Okay?"

His smile falls, "Wait, I didn't mean it like that. I trust you, I just-"

Not liking his anxiety, I quickly cut him off. "I was just joking. I know you aren't trying to hurt my feelings, and my feelings aren't hurt."

"Okay, good. I'm just not a costume kind of guy. I don't think I've worn a costume in 30 years."

My heart feels all mushy that he would wear a Viking outfit just for me with minimal complaints.

Quinn

Pacing my floor, costume on, I wait for Roni to call me over. She's over there getting dressed, and I want to see; she was acting sort of strange yesterday, so I'm a little worried. Maybe she's playing some sort of prank on me. But she isn't mean-spirited, so it can't be that bad.

What if she realizes I want her and is uncomfortable? Lead in my stomach, I peer out of the window for the billionth time this morning. Just then, my phone makes a twinkling sound, Roni's notification tone and I look to see a message telling me to come on over so she can finish up my costume. Leather pants, fur over my shoulders. What else is there? Maybe she took pity on me and got me a shirt.

I grab my wallet, hope she has a bag to keep it in since she didn't get me pants with pockets, and head over there. As I reach the front steps, Roni flings open the door, and every thought I've ever had flees my head. All I can do is stare. She is so hot. Skin-tight black leather pants, a black leather corset, faux furs like mine over her shoulders, her hair in some sort of edgy mohawk, and black make-up all around her eyes. Oh my god. Her cleavage is magnificent.

How am I ever going to keep my hands off of her?

I finally look back up at her face to see her lips pursed and eyebrow raised, then she smirks and asks, "Like what you see, big boy?" giving me a wink and a twirl.

"Roni, I'm going to say something and I don't want it to change our friendship, okay?"

Suspiciously she says, "Okay."

"You are hot as hell. Good Lord, woman, have you seen your tits in that?"

"Quinn!" She laughs, shocked.

"Nothing but the truth, ma'am. Now, are we ready to go?"

Roni, smiling, her face flushed, giggles. "Yeah, we're ready. Let me grab my bag. Do you want to take your truck or mine?" She throws a black leather bag across her shoulders.

"We can take mine. I'm going to need you to carry my wallet since I didn't get a cool Viking bag or pockets."

"Oh, my glob. I didn't even think about that!" She laugh, grabbing my wallet and putting it in her bag.

———◀O▶———

As soon as we walk into the Renaissance Faire, I relax. Roni really did a great job of picking out a getup that would let me blend in with most Faire goers. She really gets into character, changing her voice and mannerisms to suit her Viking persona, named Astrid.

"Alette!" Roni yells, "Alette! Alette! Damn it, Val!"

"Roni! Wait, um, Astrid! Shit, I forgot my own name and yours, too." They yell, pushing through the crowd. They look like Tinkerbell, in a lime green mini fairy dress with these ruffles and swoopy sleeves, blond pixie, and twinkling bells on their pointy-toed shoes.

"Hey, there Quinn!" They said excitedly, looking me up and down.

"Astrid says my name is Bjorn. It means bear."

Val pats my slightly rounded stomach and laughs. "Oh my goodness, you are such a bear!"

I slap their hand away as Roni and Val giggle together.

"Come on over to my booth and buy something!"

I groan, already lugging a large basket filled with trinkets that Roni has insisted she just needed. Obviously, she wanted less of a friend and more of a pack mule, but I am enjoying myself. Watching

Roni's excitement makes this all worth it. Well, that and this huge turkey leg that Roni bought me as soon as we walked in. I have got to figure out where to find turkeys that big so Roni can make me more. She drags me to a booth where a short man with deep brown skin, warm eyes, and a huge smile greets us. "Oh my god, is it the infamous Roni and her himbo, Quinn?"

Val gasps and slaps him on the chest, "You can't just call people himbos."

"But you said he was!"

"Not for you to repeat it!" Val says, looking sheepishly at me.

I laugh and say, "I don't even know what a himbo is."

Roni laughs so hard that I barely understand her when she says, "Pretty but dumb, like a bimbo but dude."

"Y'all think I'm pretty?" I ask before the rest of the sentence settles in, "Hey! I own my own business! A successful business, I might add! Can't be too stupid."

Roni gasps for air, clutching Val. "He just proved the point, oh my god."

When Val finally stops laughing, I say, "Now that y'all are done making fun of me, do you want to introduce me to your friend?"

"Don't worry, man. Val says I'm a himbo, too. Name's Jackson," He says, sticking his hand out.

"Infamous Himbo Quinn, at your service," I say with a laugh.

"Let's separate the himbos before they become best friends and leave us to take care of our own properties," Val says, still laughing.

I say, "I would never do that to Roni!" At the same time, Jackson says, "You pay my bills; I'm not going anywhere!"

For some reason, that sets them off more. Jackson chuckles and shakes his head.

"Come on, Bjorn, we have a joust to watch!" Roni says, taking my hand and pulling me away from a still-laughing Val and Jackson.

We weave through the crowd, her dainty hand in my large paw, until we reach a small stadium area. We climb to the top and sit down on the hard-as-hell benches. The joust begins, and Roni quickly gasps and grips my arm. I might watch her more than the show; she's laughing, pointing, and chattering, and I can barely hear any of it over my heart pounding.

Roni

Quinn has been such a trooper today, lugging a basket full of Ren Faire goodies and not once complaining. The fair is winding down, and with all the shows and competitions over for the day, all that is left are the booths and kiddie petting zoo. We wander back over to Val and Jackson's booth, where they are both sitting in camping chairs and laughing.

"How'd your first Faire go, Bjorn?" Val asks, yawning.

"Don't start that shit," Quinn grumbles around a yawn which in turn starts everyone else.

"He had more fun than he has ever had in his whole life," I pipe in, giggling. Quinn's eyes dart to me, an expression on his face that has my heart stuttering to a stop.

"Sure did, Sunflower," He smirks at me.

Val stares at Quinn for a few long seconds before saying, "We did pretty well, all of Memaw's jellies sold, and most of the other stuff we almost sold out of."

"Damn it, I was hoping to snag a blackberry jelly," I say, mournfully. Memaw makes the best blackberry jelly, and no matter how many times she shows me how to make it myself, I simply can not.

"Oh, duh! Memaw sent two specifically for you. I have them in my car. Like we'd make all this jelly and not send you some." Val rolls their eyes.

"Yes!" I fist bump Quinn who might just be more excited for the jelly than I am.

Quinn hustles around and pulls Val into his arms for a big bear hug, "Thank you. I have been waiting on some blackberry jelly coffee cake for ages."

Val squeaks as he squeezes them, making all of us laugh.

Jackson hops up, pulling Val from Quinn's arms, saying, "Don't smush the bossman, they sign my paychecks!"

Laughing, Quinn releases Val, ruffling their hair.

Chapter 14
Y'all are plotting against me.

Quinn

I have quite the lawn waste pile, so I hustle into Roni's house to see if she wants to do a bonfire tonight. Have the friends and family over, eat some food, and watch our yard trash burn. The last month or so since the Renaissance Faire has been so busy with me working overtime; I am ready to relax and have fun. The only fun I've had these past few weeks is Roni popping over every day when I get home to feed me. I find her in the kitchen making a cup of tea.

"Hey, Sunflower, you feel up to a bonfire tonight? I have so much trash in your backyard, and I need to burn it, anyway."

"Oooh! Yes! If you could run up to the store and grab some ribs, hotdogs, burgers and chips, and whatever else you can think of, that would be great. I have all the stuff for the desserts and shit."

"Of course. I'm going to catch a quick shower and head out."

"Sounds good. I'll call everyone. You want to invite your family? Or friends only? My siblings will most likely come."

"Yeah, we can invite my parents and sisters. Kids coming?"

"Of course! Most of my family wouldn't be able to come if we didn't let the kids come, too. Write your parent's number down for me. I have your sisters' already."

"Why do you have my sisters' numbers?" I ask suspiciously, my pulse racing. I don't want them to gang up on me, but Roni, being friends with my sisters, feels right. I turn away from Roni to write my parent's information on the notepad, hiding my huge smile.

"They are my newest best friends. Of course, I have their number."

"I feel like y'all are plotting against me."

"We are."

The bonfire is in full swing and my ass is parked in a lawn chair with my buddies and a cooler of beer, watching Roni, Val, Rhonda, and our collection of sisters dancing on the other side of the fire. I can't take my eyes off of Roni. Of course. Damn it. She's mine. But I can't do anything about it. She can't actually be mine. If I confess my feelings and she doesn't reciprocate, I will have ruined my favorite relationship. She is amazing and I can't risk it.

That doesn't mean I don't want to, though.

Fuck it, I have to touch her. So I prowl up behind her, grabbing her arm and spinning her towards me. A startled gasp followed by her magical giggle wraps around us as I pull her into my chest and sway to the beat. The song changes to one I recognize from a movie she made me watch, so I swing her out and back into my chest, moving my leg between hers to do a little Dirty Dancing reenacting. Roni snort-laughs as I dip her and then slowly bring her back up, staring into her gorgeous eyes. The air feels electric as we lean towards each other. Oh lord, I'm going to kiss her.

Well, I was going to kiss her. Then Val shoves between us, demanding Roni try whatever concoction Val and the sisters created. Shit smells like pure gasoline, so I wander over to where my parents are sitting, covered in grandkids, on the porch swing and grab a beer from the cooler. My mom looks like she is about to cry and my dad smirks at me.

Damn it.

They saw Roni and me dancing, almost kissing. I'm never going to live this down.

"I really like Roni; our families fit together so well. Don't you think, Quinn?" My mom says, fishing for details. I sigh, wondering just what to say to her.

"Mary, leave the boy alone. If he doesn't feel anything about her, then he just doesn't," Pops says.

Something snaps in me and I straighten my shoulders. "Damn it, that woman should be mine!" I snarl before I realize just what I said and who I snarled at. But mom looks suspiciously happy, and Pops had a smug smile, so I guess they weren't angry at the yelling.

"Shit, I didn't mean..." I say before my mom rushes over and hugs me. "Now, Ma, even if Roni and I get together and work out, she doesn't want to get married or have kids. She-" Before I can finish, my mom interrupts by telling me she just wants me happy and not dying alone.

Can't argue with that.

I open my beer and watch everyone around the bonfire; the womenfolk are tipsy, swirling, and dancing, with the children running between their legs and playing tag. The men have separated into small groups all around, chatting and nursing a beer. The unspoken rule tonight is that the women can drink all they want, and the men will get them home safe. I think they all enjoy watching the women drink and have fun; I know I am. I notice that Roni's brothers, Brian, Ant, Guy, and Troy, have separated themselves from the others and keep glancing my way, so I head over there and see what's up.

"Hey, y'all enjoying the party?" I ask, smiling.

Brian and Ant smile at me, Guy looks suspicious, and Troy straight-up scowls as they all confirm their enjoyment. I've worked with Ant before and got along with him. Brian and I were friends in high school, and we still get together occasionally. But I only met Guy and Troy tonight, not sure what I did to piss them off, but figured they'll let me know shortly.

Brian rolls his eyes at his grumpy brothers and says, "So, you and Roni, huh?"

I decide to play dumb. "What about me and Roni?"

Troy actually growls and takes a step towards me. The guy has got to be pushing 60; I don't know what I'll do if he takes a swing at me.

Ant steps forward, putting his hand on Troy's chest. "My god, Troy, calm your old ass down."

Then he turns to me. "What's up with you and Roni? We saw y'all out there dancing. Didn't particularly look friendly."

"Me and Roni are just friends. Would I like to be more? Maybe. She's a great woman. But I'm not acting on it. Our friendship is too important."

Guy looks thoughtful, and Troy says, "Good."

"Hold up," Guy says, "You're just going to give up a shot with my sister because you're scared?"

"Don't encourage him, damn it." Troy says, still glaring at me.

"V-baby is damn near 40 years old and has been completely independent for more than 20 years. What are you pissed about?" Brian says with a chuckle.

"Still my baby sister," Troy grumbles.

We all laugh, and Guy shoots a pointed look in my direction.

"Yeah, I'm scared. Do y'all know how good your sister's cooking is? If I scare her away, not only do I lose my best friend but also her amazing food. I'm not willing to risk either." I say as Sunflower's brothers all laugh.

Brian says, "I think you're making a mistake."

Then the conversation drifts away as I catch eyes with Roni from across the yard. She's smiling and surrounded by our combined sisters and Val, and she's so gorgeous that my heart skips a beat.

Roni

Soft music plays in the background as we sit on the back porch swing, watching the bonfire under the night sky. Everyone left about an hour ago, and we're both feeling a little giggly and touchy. The evening has just been perfect. After waving away the last of our friends, Quinn and I plopped down on my porch swing, not wanting to clean up just yet.

"Tonight was really fun, I didn't realize just how much I needed that," Quinn says, throwing an arm over my shoulder just as I push the swing with my foot, unbalancing me. I end up with my face resting on his chest. Knowing that I shouldn't but unable to resist I snuggle in closer to him.

I feel his chest rumble under my cheek and look up at him. His chocolate-brown eyes capture my gaze and just won't let go. Time stops as our lips touch for the very first time. The crackling fire, the music, the breeze in the trees, the crickets silenced at that moment. His hand comes up to tangle in my hair as he takes control of the kiss, our lips now crashing into each other as if we've been waiting forever for this moment.

Perhaps we have.

His tongue traces the seam of my lips, and with a sigh, I open up to him. He kisses like he does everything else, with confidence and finesse. Desire washes over me and I know just where this night will end. Hopefully, in my bed. Or his bed. Hell, the floor would do just fine.

With a broken gasp, Quinn jerks back from me, his eyes searching my face, but before he can say anything, I pull his head back down for another kiss.

Fireworks.

Gently, Quinn pulls me to straddle his lap, my dress bunched around my hips, his hands on my ass. Oh my God, I knew his lap was perfect for naughty things. His hand slides up my back to tangle his fingers in my hair as he crashes his mouth against mine.

He pulls back just enough to whisper against my lips, "How far do you want to take this tonight?"

"All the way," I say, leaning back in for another life-changing kiss before he pulls away. He stands up, letting me slide down his front, before tossing me over his shoulder with a slap on my ass.

"Quinn!" I squeal, laughing and pinching his butt through his jeans. He chuckles as he practically kicks open my door, rushing to my bedroom. He tosses me on the bed, and I bounce a couple of times before Quinn covers me with his large body. His lips find mine again as his hand travels up my body to my breast, gently, oh so gently, rubbing his thumb over my nipple. I moan into his mouth, silently begging for more pressure.

I feel him smile against my lips and murmur, "Greedy girl."

Tweaking my nipple, making me gasp and writhe against him, he plants hot open-mouthed kisses down my neck until he reaches the top of my dress. As if reminded we are still fully dressed, he pulls away from me, yanks off his shirt, and then growls, "Get naked, Sunflower, I need to see what's mine."

He rolls off of me, unbuckling his belt, and pushing his jeans down. Realizing that he can't remove his pants with his boots still on, he huffs, clearly frustrated with the amount of clothing still on his body. I giggle as I finish unbuttoning my dress and slip it off of my shoulders to pool around my feet. Quinn looks up at me, his mouth agape, as I slowly pull my boring black cotton panties down my thighs and let them drop to the floor.

"God damn, Roni. You are incredible. Just stay still a moment. I want this sight burned into my brain."

My heart seizes in my chest as my pussy clenches, but I strike a pinup-style pose and giggle at his beguiled expression.

"Come here, woman."

I step between his legs as he runs his calloused hands up and down my ass, thighs, legs, trailing fire in their wake. I moan softly, threading my fingers into his hair. My last rational thought rises to the surface and I ask, "Condom?"

"Fuck." He snarls, pressing his face into my stomach, "I don't have any, do you?"

I think quickly, weighing the pros and cons of letting Quinn go bare. Do I trust him that much? Yes, of course I do.

"I got my tubes tied a few years ago, and I haven't been with anyone since I moved here."

He smiles up at me, "I haven't been with anyone in a couple of years, myself."

"No condoms?"

His eyes take on a feral glint, "No condoms."

Quinn

Oh, my God. I am going to cum before we even get started. That body, that pose, no condoms? I get to feel everything with this woman? I have died and gone to heaven.

I pull her down to straddle me, taking her beautiful face in my hands and kissing her as if she is the air I need to survive. And, fuck, it sure feels like she is.

She rubs her soaking pussy against my hard cock, and my God, I need to taste her before I embarrass myself. I growl as I flip her onto her back. Her magical giggle wraps around my heart. Tasting my way down her neck, the indent of her collarbone, and down to those magnificent titties. More than a mouthful, more than a handful, I suck and lick all around her breast. She moans and writhes under me, begging for my mouth around her nipple. Oh no, my woman doesn't need to beg. I roughly suck her nub into my mouth. The sounds from her make my cock grow even harder, wanting relief but needing her to orgasm in my mouth. I continue working my way down her glorious body, taking my time, enjoying every gasp and whimper.

When I'm eye level with her cunt, I find myself unable to do anything but stare.

"My God, Sunflower. This is a pretty pussy, and so wet? All for me? Please let me taste you."

"Yes, you can do anything, Quinn. Anything. Just don't stop." She whines, thrusting towards my face.

"Anything?" I moan, "Oh, fuck, you can't tell me these things."

I latch on to her clit, ravenous, starved for her taste.

Lights explode behind my eyelids, vanilla and cherries. Better than anything this woman has ever cooked for me.

I feast.

Way too soon, Roni is screaming out her first release, but I haven't had enough of this perfect pussy. I slow my tongue, letting her come down gently, before slipping a finger inside of her. Letting her moans guide me, slowly I increase the pressure on her clit until her body trembles. I thrust another finger into her as I suck her nub into my mouth roughly, she yells my name as she cums for the second time.

Not yet sated but needing to be inside of her, I climb up to her mouth, notching my cock at her entrance and slowly pushing in. Her tight warm heat makes it hard to go slow, to let her get used to me. She moves, moaning, so I slow down even more. Just to tease her a bit. But when she whines, "More, Quinn, oh God, harder." I can't restrain myself anymore. I thrust wildly, grunting, hearing her get louder. I raise up enough to clasp her nipple in my mouth, lashing my tongue over the nub as she grinds her pussy against my pelvic bone, trying to get more pressure. I slide my hand between us, still tonging her nipple, and circle her clit with my finger before harshly pressing down. This time, when she screams out her orgasm, I follow behind her, filling her up with my cum.

The caveman in me beats his chest, knowing his woman is coated in him, inside and out.

I collapse against her before rolling and pulling her onto my chest. She drowsily snuggles in, smiling against my chest. Sleep starts to pull me under before I am startled by Roni shrieking, "Oh my God! Cum is dripping everywhere!"

I laugh as she penguin waddles toward the bathroom. I pat around, checking the bed for bodily fluids and finding none, follow her into the bathroom where the shower is running. Roni is tying her wild hair into a knot on the top of her head. I walk up behind her to wrap my arms around her waist and nuzzle her neck.

"Can I shower with you?"

She grins at me in the mirror. "After three orgasms, good job, by the way, you can do whatever you want to me in the shower."

I quickly spin her to face the shower and slap her on the ass, "Well, get in, woman; I'm ready to do whatever I want with you."

Then I follow that magical giggle into the steamy hot water.

Quinn

My bones pop as I stretch out and roll over, reaching for Roni only to find cold sheets and crack open my eyes. I see her in a royal blue overstuffed chair across the room, sitting with her legs crossed. She's holding a cup of tea and staring at me.

"Babe, what's wrong?" I ask, worried. Panicked almost at the thought that she might regret our night.

She smiles, thank fuck, and then says, "I really hope you don't take this the wrong way, but I need you to go home. I need today alone. Maybe tomorrow. But for sure, today."

That's a good sign. My worry deflates, but I just need to know one thing.

"Do you regret last night?"

The look of pure shock on her face does a lot to lift my dread as she rushes to set her tea on the bookshelf, climbs into the bed, and straddles me. Roni cups my cheeks and, with her mouth a mere breath away from mine, says, "Absolutely not. Last night was amazing. It's just, you're in my bed. I've never had a boy sleep in my bed before."

With a relieved sigh, I press my lips to hers, savoring the taste of tea and just plain Roni on my tongue. After a few moments, I slap her ass and say, "Well, in that case, hop up and I'll head on home. I'm meeting Kenny at the gun range in a couple hours, anyways."

She giggles, gives me one more kiss, and jumps off the bed.

"I'll make you a cup of coffee to take with you." She says as she sashays away, her ass looking amazing in the hot pink boyshort panties she has on. I love the way her ass cheeks and thighs jiggle as she struts away. It's all I can do to not tackle her in the hall just to sink my teeth right into those dimples just under where her butt cheeks meet her leg.

Roni

Jesus Christ on a cranberry cracker, that man is hot. I almost didn't want to kick him out this morning. Almost.

Thank goodness he didn't take it personally that I needed him to go. As I walk into the kitchen to feed Ginger and get Quinn's coffee going, I take stock of my emotions. No regrets, for sure. Quinn is wonderful. Everything just feels so chaotic in my head and I have to figure it out. I can't do that while looking at him.

But does he have to leave right this second? Surely there is enough time for one more orgasm. Perhaps two. So I strip out of my tank top and undies and walk back into the bedroom.

Chapter 15

As if home was on a roller coaster.

Quinn

It's been two days since I've seen Roni. Well, a day and a half but who is counting? I keep checking out the window, hoping to see her darting across my yard. Deciding to have a snack, I make my way into the kitchen and rummage through the fridge.

My front door flings open and my mouth goes dry. Damn, she's gorgeous. Her wild hair, still untamed, was forced into two braids on either side of her head and a short floral sundress, no bra. Good heavens, no bra.

She excitedly says, "Quinn Thomas Evans!"

"Wrong again, gorgeous lady."

"Damn it," Roni says, glaring at me as if my middle name is my fault as she walks towards me in the kitchen.

"What's up?" I say, making my way over to give her a kiss that releases a whole swarm of butterflies in my chest.

"Will you take me on a date?" she asks with a dreamy look. The butterflies dissipate as my chest swells with pride that I put that look on my woman's face.

"Of course, you want to go out to dinner?"

"Actually, I was wondering if it could be an overnight date at a haunted hotel?"

I bark out a laugh. That is such a Roni date idea, "Of course, when do you want to go?"

"Um, tomorrow?"

"Tomorrow? Did you already make the plans, then ask me?"

"No, of course not," she says, looking at my feet.

"You are such a dirty, rotten liar!" I say, pretending to be aghast.

She laughs and says, "Yeah, I kind of got excited. It's that hotel over in Foley, across from the tea shop where we met, you know which one?"

"Yeah, babe," I say, smirking at her. She is so damn cute.

"So it's supposed to be haunted. And I was on the website, and one thing led to another, and then, BAM! I have reservations for tomorrow!"

That damn magical giggle that I can never resist twinkles in the air like fireflies as I pull her to me again, giving her a long kiss and then a slap on the ass.

"Sounds good, Sunflower. What time is check-in? Do you have a plan for our overnight date, or do you want me to plan it?"

"Seriously? You would plan a whole day, evening, and then the next morning date? I obviously already did the hard part, the overnight part."

"Of course, I would. And thank you for doing the hard part," I say with a chuckle, giving her another kiss.

"Okay, okay, enough kisses. I need to be alone tonight. Check-in is at one but I'd like to go earlier. Make a full weekend of it."

"Sounds good. Give me your lips just one more time," I say, grabbing her hips and pulling her to me. She giggles and reaches her arms around my neck as my mouth lands on hers and the universe stops. Then, before I've had nearly enough of her, she pushes me away with a smirk.

"Text me what time we're leaving in the morning and if I need any special clothes."

A peck on the cheek and then she's gone.

I text Kenny and Brian to cancel our plans for tomorrow's shooting range trip. Then, I get to work planning a weekend date with the woman I am rapidly falling in love with.

Bright and early on Saturday morning, I ring Roni's doorbell instead of just letting myself in. This is a date, after all. I even ran down to the Walmart last night for a bouquet of wildflowers for my wildflower. She opens the door, her hair in two braids, wearing dark red pants with little suns and moons all over them and a black tank top, her ever-present Docs, and layers of jewelry that clang together like music when she moves.

"You brought me flowers! Oh, Quinn Leroy Evans, you are just wonderful!" she practically sings as she reaches for me and the flowers, giving me a kiss and dancing off with the flowers towards the kitchen. I follow behind her bellowing, "Wrong again, Wildflower!"

She giggles and says, "I like Wildflower! And these are just lovely. What are they for?"

"This is our first real date. We kind of skipped some steps. And you deserve to be surrounded by flowers. Are you packed and ready, pretty lady?"

"I am!" she squeals, as she fills a vase with water and arranges them. "What do you have planned for today?"

"Well, I thought we'd have a little brunch at the tea shop, then meander over to the used bookstore, and after that, it should be about time to check-in. After we get settled in, I figure we can stop by the ice cream shop and just walk around the park or the shops nearby. For dinner, I'm thinking we go to the Mexican restaurant. Then I figured we could roam around the hotel, hunting ghosts, and then end the night with me inside of you in our haunted hotel room."

"Oh, my goodness. Quinn. That is absolutely perfect! I'm so excited!"

"Thank fuck." I say with a laugh, the worry releasing from my shoulders. I thought I had made the right plan for Roni, but what if I was wrong, and she wanted fancy? But I should have known better. This is my Roni, after all.

"What are we doing with your little bloodthirsty demon?" I ask, still not over our vet adventure.

"We're just leaving her here. Val is going to come over and feed her tonight and in the morning."

"Poor Val. We'll have to bring them a nice treat to make up for the horror we're putting them through," I say as I grab Roni's bag and head to my bike.

"Oh, shut up. Ginger doesn't deserve a bit of this hate that you and Val give her. She is just my sweet little angel baby." Roni says, planting kisses all over the demon cat's face. I swear Ginger is smirking at me.

As I'm putting Roni's luggage in my saddlebag, she squeals, "We're taking the bike? This is the best date ever!"

Roni

The ride to the hotel was wonderful. I love being on the back of Quinn's bike, the sun on my face, wind in my hair. Sure, it's a tangled mess now, even though I had it in braids. But the time on the bike is worth the knots I'll have to brush out later. We leave the bike at the hotel and walk to the tea shop, hand in hand, my heart racing. His eyes meet mine as he holds open the door, and my whole body tingles. I've never had this reaction to another person, this feeling of excitement and electricity mixed with comfort. It's as if home was on a roller coaster.

We order and have a seat, Quinn's large body looks even more massive next to the delicate tea sets and tiny tables.

"I hope none of this shit is too expensive. I just know that I am going to knock something over and break it. I'm not trying to spend a whole paycheck on broken cups."

I laugh and say, "Nah, everything is reasonably priced. Just sit down. I'll do all the getting up so you don't have to risk it."

"Now, I can't let you do that. We're on a date, I handle everything."

"No, you pay for everything. I can get napkins and forks and stuff."

"We'll see." He says with a wink that makes my stomach flutter.

After finishing up with brunch, we walk over to the used book-store where I quickly abandon Quinn at the Westerns and find myself in the romance section. After just a few minutes, I have a rather large stack of books sitting at my feet when I hear Quinn yell, "Where is my wife? I'm looking for my wife!" I roll my eyes, laughing, as the lady at the counter shushes him with a glare. He looks properly abashed and heads in my direction.

"Well, fancy meeting you here, cowboy," I say with a giggle, gestur-ing to his handful of westerns. He quickly scoops up my haul and asks, "Are you done looking? It's 1:30. I figured it was about time to mosey across the road."

"Yep, I'm done. Give me my books and we can check out."

"No, ma'am. As you said, this is a date and as such, I pay for everything. You might as well have left your wallet at home. It's useless this weekend."

"But I can not let you buy my books. I have like 20," I say, making grabby hands at my stack of books in his large arms.

He just laughs and walks to the still-glaring cashier. I pull my debit card out and stand in front of the machine, waiting to sneak it in and pay. When the lady says the total, I start to insert my card, but

Quinn wraps his arms around me, lifts me up, and deposits me on the other side, the debit card still in hand.

Damn it.

"Nice try, Sunflower," Quinn says with a smile.

"Next time," I say as menacingly as possible with a smile on my face. He leans over and kisses my temple, and warmth spreads through my chest.

"Just let me do this. I want this date to be just right. That includes paying for everything. Okay, wifey-dear?" he asks, making puppy dog eyes at me.

How am I supposed to resist that? "Fine, fine. You win. I will leave my wallet in the room unless I need my license?"

"If you want a margarita, you will need it, but I can put it in my wallet," he says, grabbing my hand and the bag of books.

Once we're checked in, we go up the stairs, taking in the antiques and red brocade curtains, into our room. Quinn settles our bags next to the dark wood four-poster bed, while I check out the bathroom with its claw-foot tub and pink tiles. The toilet flushes on its own, causing me to jump and really need to use the scary toilet.

"Quinn?"

"Yeah, babe," He says, walking through the open door of the bathroom and looking at me.

"Could you just like, sit on the toilet for a second?"

"Sure. Why?" He asks as he sits on the toilet.

"Because that damn thing flushed on its own and I wanted to make sure nothing was going to come up and bite me in the ass while I pee."

"So you'll sacrifice my ass to save yours?"

"Yes."

"Good girl." He says, standing up, grinning at me, leaving me alone in the bathroom with a "Go pee," thrown over his shoulder.

I handle my business, wash my hands, fling open the door, and jump onto the bed. Quinn laughs and jumps beside me, leaning over to kiss me, softly. As he deepens the kiss, I push him back. "Sir! What kind of girl do you take me for? We haven't even finished our first date and you're already trying to get into my pants?"

Quinn lets out a loud guffaw, as he hop up and pulls me off the bed, "Pardon me, ma'am."

"That's better."

Chapter 16
Hunt a ghost.

Quinn

With Roni's soft hand in mine, we walk down to the ice cream shop, debating the best ice cream flavors and whether a cone or a cup is better. Cone, obviously, but Roni decides to be completely wrong and asks for a cup. Which I guess is fine since she wanted hot fudge. I wouldn't want her to get burned. That would ruin our first date.

Settling on a bench and finishing our ice cream, we sit there chatting about everything and nothing at all. It is an absolutely perfect way to spend the afternoon. We lose track of time, spending hours, telling stories from our childhood and the past twenty years. The sun starts to set, I realize with a jolt, and my ass is numb from sitting on this bench for damn near four hours.

"Well, my dear, I think it's time we head on over to the Mexican restaurant and have dinner," I say, standing and reaching out to pull Roni up.

"Shit, hold on," she says, grimacing. "My foot is asleep." She slowly rotates her foot, a sour expression on her face. I wait until she stops moving her foot, boop her on the nose, my heart stopping at her magical giggle and grab her hand, walking towards the restaurant.

I hold the door open for Roni to walk in, getting a little peek at that ass as she walks in front of me. She looks over her shoulder, giving me a sexy smirk, and I just wink at her. The hostess gives a bright smile to Roni before turning to me, her eyes trailing up and down my body, making me uncomfortable. Roni threads her arm through mine as we are led to our seats. Roni slides in the booth first, and I sit on the same side, wanting to be near her. Without sparing a glance for Roni, the hostess hands me the menus and tells me she hopes I enjoy my meal. I glance at Sunflower, hoping she isn't upset but find her barely containing a laugh. When we make eye contact, she snort-laughs, saying, "She wanted to eat you alive, hottie."

"She made me uncomfortable."

"I don't know if I should be happy that you are the kind of guy you are or if I should go fist-fight her for making you uncomfortable," Roni says with a laugh.

"Awe, you'd defend my honor?"

"Any day of the week."

My god, I am in love with this woman. This realization does not cause panic; it just gives me a feeling of rightness and joy.

But then the fear sets in. What if she doesn't love me? What if I am just another Polaroid for her wall? Damn it, it never occurred to me that this might be just like her other relationships to her. I'm all in and she might never be.

I feel her squeeze my hand and look into her eyes, realizing two things at the same time, the first is that she already has love in her eyes when she looks at me. A softness that isn't there for anyone else.

And the second is that she must have called my name a few times because she looks exasperated as she asks, "Quinn?"

"Sorry, Sunflower. Your beauty distracted me."

She laughs. "You are ridiculous. Could you let me out? I need to go to the restroom."

"Of course," I say, standing and helping her out.

I pull out my phone, ignoring the ache in my chest that seems to always be there when Roni isn't near, and answer a few work emails. I'm scrolling through social media when I feel someone approach. Looking up, expecting to see Roni or our server, I find the hostess standing there, smiling seductively. She leans over, takes a napkin from the table, and writes her number on it. She says, "Call me sometime." As she slides the napkin in front of me. Grinding my teeth, I push the napkin back over to her and say, "No, I will not be calling you. I am in love with my girlfriend and would never do that to her."

The hostess's facial expression changes to anger quickly, but before she can open her mouth, Roni is there, tapping her on the shoulder, "Excuse me, my boyfriend just declared his love for me and I would like to enjoy it. Run along now."

I'm stunned. I can't believe she heard me. Can't believe I confessed my love for her to a woman hitting on me instead of to my Sunflower.

"Do you think I could sit with you, big boy?" Roni asks with a giggle, and I realize I've just been staring at her beautiful face. I silently stand up, letting her scoot into the booth, before turning to face her.

"Roni, I'm so sorry. I should have told you first, not her. I shouldn't have said it out of anger. I-"

She cuts me off with a finger to my lips. "Now, hush. I love that you told her in no uncertain terms that you were off the market. I am not upset at all."

"I love you," I say, looking into her green eyes.

Her eyes fill with tears, and she leans over and kisses me. Fireworks fill my chest as I deepen the kiss, holding her face until I hear an impatient throat clearing behind me.

The server looks positively put out as she says, "What can I get y'all to drink tonight?"

Roni giggles and says, "Sorry about that. Your hostess hit on him and he turned her down. It was hot."

Our server, Jamie, according to her name tag, sighs and says, "Ugh, yeah. All that girl does is try to find a man, your man, my man, any man will do."

I chuckle while Roni becomes best friends with Jamie before finally letting the woman take our drink orders.

"Why'd you get water?" I ask as soon as Jamie leaves.

Roni looks at me, her heart in her eyes, and says, "You just told me you love me. I want to remember every minute of tonight."

I feel so light I could just float away. To keep me on the ground, I grab Roni's hand and kiss her knuckles, telling her I love her in between kisses. Her shining eyes tell me all that I need to know about her feelings. She loves me, and once she identifies that feeling and comes to terms with it, she will tell me. Until then, I will shower her with affection.

Roni

My heart races as we stroll, my hand in his, toward the hotel. I'm so happy I could burst but panicked that I don't think I can fall in love. Quinn is wonderful, and I enjoy him in my home. He makes my heart race, has a masterful dick, and I want to see him almost every day.

I take a deep breath and release, letting my panic float away on the music-filled breeze.

"Where is that music coming from?" I ponder, looking around.

"Dunno. Want to follow it and see?"

"Oh, yes! What fun!"

We meander in the direction of the music, around the corner from the hotel into the courtyard. A country band is playing a love song while a bunch of couples slow dance on the cobblestone.

Quinn grins down at me before offering me his hand, "Wanna dance, pretty lady?"

I giggle before taking his hand and letting him swing me into his chest. We sway to the music getting lost in each other's arms. When the band plays an uptempo song, breaking the spell, Quinn laughs and runs his fingers through my hair, well, more like gets his fingers tangled in my windblown hair and pulls my head back, looking me in the eyes as he leans down to kiss me. The kiss is gentle but full of his love and devotion and has my heart racing. Then he pulls back, smiles, slaps my ass and says, "Let's go hunt a ghost or two."

I giggle as he grabs my hand and drags me back to the hotel.

We spend the next two hours roaming the public parts of the hotel, laughing, kissing, and scaring ourselves until the front desk lady tells us we're being too loud. We rush upstairs, like two naughty children, giggling, and burst into our room, out of breath and with our cheeks aching from smiling so much.

Chapter 17

Looks like a fairy, walks like bigfoot.

Roni

I let myself into Quinn's house, my bucket of cleaning supplies in hand. Quinn is super neat, so I only have to come to his house once a week to vacuum, clean the bathroom, and do those sorts of things. I try to do the cleaning over here while he is at work because it stresses him out to have me cleaning while he sits around. He'll get up and help, even with me protesting. So I sneak over while he is at work, and the next day, he always shows up with a huge bouquet and tons of sour gummies as a thank you. I'm scrubbing under his toilet when I hear his front door open.

"I'm in here!" I yell since he didn't know I would be here.

"I figured you were somewhere since I went to your house first. Come give me a kiss," He says, walking down the hall. I stand up and say, "Let me wash my hands first. I'm pretty gross."

"Whatcha doing?" He asks, leaning against the bathroom door.

"Just the weekly cleaning," I reply, scrubbing my hands.

"I need to talk to you about that, actually."

He pulls me to him and gives me a quick kiss, then says, "I don't want you cleaning my house anymore."

"Why not? Am I not doing a good enough job?" I ask, my throat tight.

"What? No, no, you are wonderful. I just, it makes me uncomfortable having my girlfriend clean my house."

"But you still do the upkeep on my house. I don't see why our deal has to change just because we are dating."

"But all of that seems like boyfriend duties, you know? I'll beg you to keep cooking for me, but the cleaning seems too far. I don't want to take advantage of our relationship."

I laugh. "You aren't taking advantage of me or our relationship. I would like to keep our original agreement. You do all of my upkeep and the nonsense I don't want to handle, I do your cooking and cleaning. I feel good about this trade, can't you?"

"If you are positive that you feel good about it, then I can be okay with it. But if you ever want to stop cleaning my house, please let me know. Promise?"

"I'll even pinky-promise," I say, holding out my little finger. He chuckles, intertwines his finger with mine, and says, "Deal."

"Alright, go play outside, and let me finish here."

"I'm not a toddler, Roni."

"The faster you get out from under my feet, the faster I can get done and start cooking your dinner."

"Okay, Ma! Flash the porch light when you want me to come back inside." He says, making both of us laugh. He grabs the back of my neck, pulls me in for a hard kiss, and leaves the bathroom. I hear him grabbing a guitar from his living room wall and he goes out to his front porch, playing some of my favorite songs. Heat rushes around my heart as I finish cleaning his bathroom, my mind on the man just outside.

My pounding heart drowns out the sounds of guitar as I change his sheets. I think of the last few months since our relationship became romantic and how perfect everything is. We spend a few nights together and then a few nights apart. We do most things together but make time for our friends. Our families love each other.

I'm terrified.

It's been almost a year since we met, and nothing good stays in my life much longer than that. I don't know what I was thinking, letting us go this far. We should have stayed friends so I can keep him in my life.

And I desperately want this man in my life.

I think I need to be alone tonight.

I can feel myself start to spiral and need to get home before Quinn sees me break down.

I quickly put away all the cleaning supplies and his dirty sheets in the hamper and follow the music to the porch and Quinn. He stops playing as I step outside, the smile on his face dimming at whatever he sees on mine.

"What's wrong, Sunflower?" He asks, snagging my hand and pulling me onto his lap. I try to push away, but his strong arms won't budge.

I shrug, laying my head on his strong chest, tears welling in my eyes.

"Talk to me. I thought you were fine earlier. What happened? Do you want to stop cleaning my house but don't know how to tell me?" He asks, concern wrapped around his words.

I laugh and sniffle, "No," I mumble into his chest.

"Did you find something in my house that upset you?"

"No," I mumble again.

"Babe, you're going to have to give me a hint. I'm freaking out a little bit here."

I sigh, pull my head from his chest, and feel the tears fall down my face.

"I'm just, I don't know. Like, relationships don't last in my life. Except for Val and my siblings. Everyone else eventually gives me claustrophobia or something. You're my favorite relationship. What if that happens with you? Oh, my god. What if it doesn't? What if you get bored with me? What if you leave me, like my mom and dad? We shouldn't have done this, we should have just stayed friends. I don't want to lose you." I sob out, unable to control my breathing as panic overwhelms me.

"Hey, hey, hey," He says, looking into my eyes, "Breathe with me, babe. In, out..."

I slowly sync my breathing with his, and my heart rate slows.

"Listen to me, Sunflower. You are it for me. I am in love with you. Even if you can never say that back to me, you are still mine. In my heart, you will always be mine. If you feel claustrophobic and need to run, then run. Just come back home to me when you're done. And leave a note or something, so I don't panic and think you've been kidnapped. Just talk to me, and we can figure it all out. You aren't on your own anymore. Let me help you calm your mind."

His words wrap around my heart and squeeze until it's almost painful.

"Thank you," I say, my voice trembling.

"Don't thank me for being here for you. That's my job. Now, are you good?"

"I am."

"In that case, are you still cooking, or do you want me to run into town for dinner?"

I crack up, this man and his food.

"Let me take a shower, and then I'll cook," I say, giggling and kissing his cheek. He turns his head, catches my lips, and slowly plunders my mouth, his hands fisted in my hair.

"Want me to join you?" He asks, pulling away from my mouth.

"Yes, but you can't. Not if you want dinner."

He sighs and gives me pitiful eyes. "But I'm going to miss you so much."

"Oh, shush you." I say, laughing, "Why don't you chop the vegetables for me? Then all I have to do is cook the meat when I get out of the shower."

"Sounds good, babe."

The sunlight filtering in through the sheer curtains and trails of ivy warms my face as I slowly wake up, wrapped in Quinn's strong arms. Peace, one thing I've never been able to reach, wraps my heart up in contentment. I shift a bit so I can see his face, partially covered in his reddish-brown beard. His nose is strong and his eyebrows could really use a plucking.

I wonder if he'll let me.

But I know he will.

Since our relationship veered into the romantic lane, he has shown me nothing but devotion. Before that, he was fantastic and caring, even from the moment I met him.

He shifts in his sleep, tugging me closer, and breathes out, "Go back to sleep, Sunflower, I love you."

I love you, too. My brain screams, but the words won't form in my mouth. I'm going to mess this up, I just know it. Why can't I just say the words? I feel them. This man has such a grip on my heart and yet, I can't acknowledge it? I can't tell him?

He deserves so much better than me.

"Calm down, Sunflower. I know you love me, too. I don't need the words."

And with that bomb, the asshole falls right back to sleep and starts snoring.

I should make a cup of tea.

I crawl over this magnificent man, his hands roaming my body even in sleep, and slowly make my way into the kitchen, grabbing lost teacups on my way. Once I have a cup of tea ready, I work on buttermilk biscuits. I toss those into the oven, set a timer, and place the first slice of bacon in my cast iron, knowing it will only be minutes before the smell wakes Quinn. Sure enough, before it's even time to flip the meat, Quinn's strong arms surround me as he kisses my neck murmuring, "Good morning, Sunshine. Breakfast smells amazing."

I turn in his arm to kiss him, smiling against his lips, "Go take your shower. Breakfast will be ready soon. Then I want to spend the day alone, but maybe have a late lunch?"

"Sounds perfect. I have some husbandly duties to attend to, mainly buying a new lawnmower because yours sucks."

"Oh, it's just finicky." I giggle, his affection pouring over me.

"Sure, woman, sure." He smiles, slaps my ass, and walks back to the bedroom.

I finish cooking the bacon and then drop the eggs into the bacon grease to fry while I get the coffee going. I salt, pepper, and season with Slap Ya Mama. Then, I flip. The biscuit timer dings just as Quinn walks into the kitchen, chest bare and hair damp. He sees me staring, smirks, and turns the timer off. Blushing and giggling, I take the biscuits out and plate up our breakfast.

Quinn grabs the plates from me and places them on the table. "Sit down, baby. I'll pour the coffee."

He fixes my coffee exactly how I like it, with a ton of flavored creamer and absolutely no sugar. He kisses my forehead and sits across from me to eat. We chat around mouthfuls of bacon and eggs about everything and nothing at all. Those three all-important words are bubbling up to the surface, but I'm still unable to actually get them out. I watch his dear face as he super-duper enjoys his breakfast, allowing his calming presence to soothe me.

When we finish, Quinn grabs our plates to wash, but I stop him, "You go on, I'll wash them later."

"Alright, babe. I'll see you in a little bit," He says, kissing my forehead.

A few hours later, I'm tending my sorely neglected garden. Goodness, it's a mess. I've been so wrapped up in Quinn that I've forgotten about my poor vegetables. Luckily, my sunflowers, which Quinn has not killed, are doing great. Dirt up to my elbows, coating the knees of my overalls, my brain tumbling over my relationship with Quinn. A basket with tomatoes, cucumbers and way too much zucchini sits next to me while a 90s playlist serenades me from my phone. A gust of wind brings the scent of honeysuckles as it whips my hair around my face.

The crunching of tires alerts me to Quinn's arrival back home and the urge to run to him is almost overwhelming. I control myself, but just barely. I need my alone time, gosh darn it!

I glance up and see Quinn strolling towards me with a huge smile, which makes my heart skip a beat.

"Hey, Sunflower!"

"No!" I bark out.

That stops him in his tracks. He tilts his head to the side like a confused golden retriever and laughs.

"Yes, ma'am. When can I come back?"

"Give me three more hours and we'll have a picnic."

"Sounds good, babe. Can I give you a kiss?"

"Absolutely not."

Quinn

Lunch devoured, Roni and I are snuggled up on a blanket in her yard. Situated between her sunflower patch and the woods, it's like we're in our own little world.

"You know what would be fun?" I whisper in Roni's ear, "If you'd let me chase you through the woods and fuck you where I catch you."

"It's sweet that you think you could catch me," my Sunflower says playfully. I lean over to whisper more naughty things in her ear, but she hops off the blanket and takes off running for the woods.

What is she doing? She isn't...fuck; she is. All the blood rushes to my cock as I take off running after her. No way am I letting this moment escape. She disappears into the treeline and I slow down so I can listen for her footsteps. She might look like some fairy from the woods, but she walks like a bigfoot. As soon as she moves, I'll know where she is.

Minutes go by as I silently roam about the treeline becoming more and more feral and needy as I do.

"Sunflower, where are you?" I sing-song out, knowing she can't resist a bit of goofiness. And sure enough, her magical giggle rings out to my left and I prowl that way. When I get close, I intentionally let myself step on a stick, a warning for her. Just as I hoped she would, she takes off running, but I'm right behind her, and before she takes more than a couple of steps, I have my arms around her and thrust her roughly against the tree. Her whimpering gasp and blown pupils are the hottest thing I've ever seen. I clasp both of her arms above her head with one hand and my other snatches my belt off. Her lips yield to mine in an earth-shattering kiss. I trail hot, open-mouthed kisses from her lips, down her neck to her breasts. Through her tank top, I tug at a nipple with my teeth. She yelps and I chuckle darkly, wrapping my belt around her arms and onto a low-hanging branch.

"Comfortable?" I ask against her strawberry lips. She moans and I pull away. "Answer with words, love. I will not have you in pain."

She whispers a yes, but that's not good enough. I grab her chin, look straight into her eyes, and demand, "Tell me you are comfortable and that you feel no strain on your arms or anywhere else."

"Goddamn it, yes. I am comfortable and not strained. Fuck."

"Oh yes, I will definitely fuck you," I say as I grind my throbbing cock against her. She gasps against my mouth just before I slam my lips to hers.

I then slide down her and drop to my knees. I slowly run my hands up her thigh and then suddenly she's gone. Running farther into the woods, giggling, as I jump to my feet and take off after her.

After a couple of minutes, her clomping steps are silent. Not a giggle to be heard, so I stop running, listening. Leaves crunch to my right, followed by a magical giggle, so I silently stalk towards the sound. She sees me coming and with a squeal, tries to run, but I catch her and push her against the tree. She isn't getting away from me this time. I push her skirt up and, finding her wet, I unbuckle my pants and she slides to her knees, finishing the job. I rip my shirt off. "Here, baby," I gasp. "Put this under your knees."

She barely has my cock out before she swallows it all the way to the back of her throat. I start gently pumping as she grabs my ass, encouraging me to go faster. I let loose, using her face like a pussy, her fingertips digging into my ass. I look down at her, not wanting to miss a single second of this, and see her right hand slide down her body to flick her clit. The sight of her fucking herself has me ready to blow, so I snatch her up, push her against the tree, and replace her hand with mine. She moans into my mouth as I add another finger.

"Fuck me, Quinn," She whines into my mouth.

"Not until you come," I growl, dropping to my knees, thrusting a third finger inside of her as I suck her clit into my mouth. Her hips gyrating, I lick, suck, slurp until her knees are shaking and she is clenching down on my fingers. "Quinn!" she screams as she comes, the most beautiful sound on earth, her shattering under my mouth and on my fingers.

I stand up, flipping her around, giving her a second to steady herself against the tree, before ramming into her with a shout. I set a brutal pace, pounding, grabbing, so close. I reach around, slap her clit, bite her shoulder, and apply pressure, feeling her come again. I let loose, barely holding her up as my blood redistributes itself throughout my body.

"Fuck, Sunflower, I'm dizzy."

She giggles as I pull out and yank up my jeans, kissing her as I help her fix her skirt and tank top. I pull her to me, just to hold her for a minute, my face pressed against her neck, still breathing heavily.

"I love you so much," I whisper into her ear, feeling her melt against me. Pulling back, I look her in the eye, "I know you love me, too. I feel it in my soul. As long as I have you, I don't need anything else."

She pulls me to her for a slow kiss, so charged with emotion that I can barely breathe. We pull apart, and she smiles at me, bending over to grab my shirt off the ground. As soon as she has my shirt, I toss her over my shoulder with a slap on the ass. Her snort-laugh, the reason I love to carry her this way, wraps itself around my heart, giving me that last burst of energy needed to carry her out of the woods. Once we get back to her yard, I sit her down and lean against her. "Whew, baby. I need a nap."

She laughs, "Me too."

We walk, hand in hand, into her house and collapse into the bed. She snuggles right up to me and yawns, "After our nap, I'll cook you dinner, but then you need to go home. I feel like I need a few days this time."

God, I love how she tells me exactly what she needs.

Chapter 18
Dog in a tux.

Roni

Noticing that Val's car isn't in the driveway I knock on the door before opening it to let Memaw know I'm here.

"It's just me!" I holler through the doorway.

"I'm in the kitchen, girl."

Memaw is standing at the stove stirring a big pot of something that smells incredible. Her gnarled hands grip the wooden spoon as she turns to face me, amusement in her eyes but no smile on her face.

"So, Valentine tells me that a fellow managed to snag you. How'd that happen?"

I belt out a laugh at her straightforward question, "Something like that. He's sweet and charming and leaves me the fuck alone when I tell him to. It's marvelous."

She harrumphs before saying, "You should bring him over sometime. Let me scare him off."

"If I haven't scared him off yet I doubt you will. He's different than the others."

"Has to be, I guess, to get your attention. Well, that's alright, then. I guess you came for more blackberry jelly. I just put some up yesterday."

"You are an absolute angel of a lady."

"Don't try to bullshit a bullshitter," Memaw grumps. "Now, I've got a box of jellies and some apple butter over on the deep freeze. You take that to your sister and let me finish this batch of peaches."

"Yes, ma'am. Tell Val I stopped by," I say, grabbing the box.

"Hey, V-baby, you just caught me. I've got about an hour before I have to head to an appointment," Janie says, holding open her screened door for me to slide through. I set her box of goodies on her black marble kitchen island, taking in the whole modern vibe of her kitchen. Such a stark contrast to mine without a plant in sight and all black and white. I dig it but wouldn't want to cook in it.

Janie, never one to rest while things need doing, starts putting away the jams and preserves. "Want some coffee and a donut?"

"Did you make or buy the donuts?"

"Made, of course. I had the kids this past weekend, and you know they demand the homemade ones," Janie replies, tucking a silver strand behind her ear. Janie and I have the same face, but that is where our similarities end. My sister is casually elegant, wearing fitted jeans and a white T-shirt with her hair in a sleek bob. I spent years trying to emulate her before realizing I just don't have that particular bit of DNA.

Janie bustles around the kitchen, making coffee and putting together a little snack for us. When I see what is on her tray I laugh, "I can not believe you still have my dishes!"

"Of course, I do. You need something to eat off of when you come over."

"I'm not 14 anymore, I can eat off of boring white dishes now," I reply, still laughing.

"Oh shush. My V-baby gets her special plate even if she is 40."

My eyes prick with tears, damn, getting all loved up is making me weepy. When I moved in with Janie after the death of our parents she had this immaculate life. And the poor woman had a tornado of a teenager thrust upon her all-white apartment. I came covered in grief and with mismatched suitcases. I cried every mealtime because everything was so bare and empty but I just couldn't express the problem. Finally, Janie took me to the thrift store and let me pick out my own dishes, throw pillows, and a weird statue of a dog wearing a tux. My constant crying stopped and I really loved living with Janie.

She still has that statue on her front porch.

Instead of replying, I shove a bite of pastry into my mouth while Janie softly smiles at me. She always knows when my emotions are getting to me and quickly changes the subject. "What's Quinn up to today?"

"I actually don't know. I haven't seen him in a couple days. We'll get together tonight." I reply with an exaggerated wink.

Janie throws her white cloth napkin at my face, "Gross."

I throw it back at her, "Only to you."

"Whatever, you have a whole family of folks that would be grossed out by your sex life."

"So I guess I shouldn't tell you how I got all of these scratches on my legs," I say with a smirk.

She leans over to look at my legs under the table, sighs, and says, "Fine. I'll bite. How'd you get the scratches on your legs?"

"Well, it involves me and Quinn, naked and running through the woods."

"I really regret asking. That is way more than I wanted to know about your sex shenanigans," Janie says, grimacing.

"I never said it was a sex thing!"

Janie doesn't hold back her laugh, "You can not expect me to believe that you had Quinn running through the woods with his dick swinging and ya'll didn't do anything nasty."

"But I never *said* that!"

Janie rolls her eyes. "A rose by any other name..." she trails off before hopping up. "Oh! I went digging around in my attic and found that box of Momma's jewelry and hair things, I think the last time I saw it was when I moved into this house before you left. You want me to snag it so you can plunder?"

"Oh my, yes! You promised me some of those pieces years ago!"

"I know! But you never reminded me!" Janie yells over her shoulder as she rushes down the hall. Minutes later she returns with a box that makes my heart seize in my chest. Momma's box. It's a light wicker, fraying along the edges, with an elaborate emerald greed latch and matching silk lining the inside.

Nostalgia hangs thick in the air as we open the box, which, given our reverence, might as well glow gold.

My eye first catches on my mother's hair combs, which are plentiful and in all colors and styles. Momma had wild hair like me and kept it off her face with French combs and bobby pins. When I think of my mother, I think of her in the sunlight, her hair glittering with jewels.

"You should take all of the combs, you're the only one that would get use from them," Janie says, patting my hand.

"Oh, I couldn't, what if-" I stammer before Janie interrupts me.

"You can and you will. No one else will use them and they shouldn't spend the next twenty years locked in a box. I should have given them to you ages ago."

"Are you sure? Shouldn't we check with everyone else?" I ask.

"Listen to me, they're yours. No one is going to say anything different. Let me go grab a bag to put them in for you."

When she leaves the room a simple white gold chain grabs my attention.

I want it. I don't even have a pendant for it or wear necklaces but this one feels like mine.

"I'm keeping this chain, too!" I yell in the empty kitchen.

"What chain?" Janie asks walking into the room with a simple white tote bag.

"Who has white tote bags? Don't they get dirty?"

"What are you doing to your tote bags?" Janie asks, head tilted.

"Using them!"

Janie just shakes her head and laughs, "Want me to get you a grocery bag instead?"

"No, this'll be fine. I want this chain," I say, dangling my new piece of jewelry in front of Janie's face.

"Okay, you can have it. Want one of the pendants for it?"

"Nope. Just this and the combs."

"Alright, so, oh! Shit! I've got to go!" Janie hops up, rushing around the table to kiss my cheek and says, "Lock up when you leave."

And then she's gone, her lavender perfume lingering in the air.

Chapter 19

It's you, me, that damn cat, and our two houses against the world.

Roni

It's late at night and we're cuddled up in bed, just talking about our last few days. Candles lend a warm dreamy quality to the room. One of my favorite parts of alone time is catching each other up and just enjoying being in each other's arms again.

"I have a question," I say, suddenly feeling nervous.

"Shoot," Quinn says, running his fingertips up and down my side.

"Just curious when you actually started to like-like me? It was the bonfire, right?"

He laughs, "Like-like you? Oh no, dear, I fell in love with you while you were singing karaoke. I mean, I was already hurtling that way since the moment I laid eyes on you climbing out of your jeep at that tea place. But that night at the bar, my heart claimed you as mine. Of course, I couldn't admit it then. But like a bolt of lightning on our date, it finally sunk in that I was in love with you."

My heart can't take it. I lean over and kiss him, trying to show him without the words I can't seem to say, just how much I love him, too.

He kisses me back, just as he loves me, unrestrained and all-consuming. His hands slowly trail up and down my body, soft, and full of love.

Roni

I'm curled up in my double papasan chair, cuddling with Ginger and reading a sappy, emotion-filled book, when Quinn lets himself into my living room. I smile up at him as he leans over to kiss me.

"Well, hello there, handsome. Have a good day at work?"

"I did. How was your day, my dear?" He asks, picking my legs up so he can sit down.

"Pretty alright. I finished my project this morning, so I just puttered around."

"Nice. Kenny was talking about going to the bar tonight. Want to get together a combined boys' and ladies' night? Maybe they'll pull the karaoke machine out again," Quinn says, wiggling his eyebrows.

I laugh, a plan hatching in my mind, as I say, "Sounds good. I'll call Rhonda and figure it all out."

Why am I so damn nervous? It's just karaoke. I sang horribly in this bar just a few months ago. Never been scared before. Pull it together. If you cry on stage, you'll never hear the end of it. The only thing I have going for me on that stage is confidence. Shit. I don't even have to do this. Quinn doesn't know what I planned. I can lean over right now and whisper, 'I love you,' and not do this.

No. Screw that. He deserves a big gesture, and I know he will love it. Just because I'm a little nervous doesn't mean I get to bitch out now.

Breathe in.

Breathe out.

My turn is up next, so I lean over and whisper in Quinn's ear, "This next song is for you. Listen to the words. They are all for you."

Watching his eyes light up, I know I've made the right choice.

Quinn

For me? Damn. My heart races as I watch my girl head up to the stage and whisper her selection to the DJ. As he gets her music selection up, our table erupts into applause. All the cheers fade away as the most perfect woman walks on stage and the opening strains of a love song that was popular in the 90s play. My heart feels so full that it just might burst. Wouldn't that be some shit? The woman of my dreams poorly sings me a song and I just die.

I'm love-struck through the song's opening, unable to do anything but stare at Roni as she looks straight into my eyes. When she gets to the chorus and sings those three magical words straight into my heart, I jump out of my seat.

My heart is pounding, and I can't wait another moment to touch that magnificent woman. She hasn't even finished the song when I rush onto the stage, the bright lights blinding me for a moment. I grab the love of my life and throw her over my shoulder. Her laughter is the oxygen I breathe—no, more necessary than that. I crave that musical sound, and knowing that I caused it makes me want to beat my chest, caveman style.

"Quinn, what are you doing?" She asks breathlessly as I storm out of the front door and into the parking lot. I'm too overcome to speak as I place her gently on her feet. Her back is against her Jeep, and I press against her until I can feel every inch of her against me.

"Tell me." I beg roughly against her neck, "Say it. Tell me you love me."

"I love you, Quinn." She whispers in my ear.

The world tilts under my feet, and I have never been this happy or horny ever in my life. I've got to taste her. Now. I slide my hands under her skirt to grip her delectable ass as I hit my knees. I place wet, sloppy kisses up her thigh until my head is under her skirt and my mouth is over her weeping mound. Her smell is intoxicating, and I know I will never get enough of her. I rip her thong off and ravenously suck her clit into my mouth. Her loud moan makes me pause. "Honey, you've got to be quiet, or we're both going to jail." She whimpers as I hungrily put my mouth back where it belongs - on her pussy.

Roni

I'm wrapping up a dreadfully dull work project when I hear Quinn's guitar outside. I fling open my front door, seeing him sitting on his porch, grinning at me. I wave and he transitions into playing one of my favorite songs. I lean against my door frame with my heart in my throat, I really do love this man.

A sliver of anxiety runs down my spine as I push away from the door and walk through the house into my bedroom. Intent on doing some gardening, I change into my pink overalls and throw my hair into a bun—or something like a bun. I look startlingly similar to a pineapple. I simply have way too much uncontrollable hair to do cute, messy buns.

In the sunroom, I slide my feet into my gloriously ugly lime green Crocs and grab my bucket of gardening tools. My heart is pounding and waves of anxiety wash over me as this claustrophobic feeling crushes my ribcage. I want to run, grab Ginger and go. As soon as that thought crosses my mind grief hits me, so hard that my eyes fill with tears. Leaving Quinn would be devastating.

Focus.

Breathe.

Don't spiral.

Fuck, I need to talk to Quinn. I need to make sure that we are on the same page. If we aren't, maybe we can still salvage our friendship.

Oh, God. What have we done? What if I lose him?

I stomp over to his house, following the sound of guitar strings.

"Quinn, we need to talk," I say, my panic reaching a crescendo as I storm up his front steps and completely interrupt his guitar playing. I love listening to him play as I work in my garden, but we need to talk about this being in love deal. He said it. I said it. We are seeing only each other. But this is where all of my other relationships went wrong.

Oh, not the love part.

I've only ever loved Quinn, but the cohabitation. They always expect more and I don't want it. I want my house that no man has ever lived in, but I want that with Quinn next door.

He grins up at me, his brown hair shimmering auburn in the sun, "Okay, babe. Shoot."

"I don't want to get married."

He chuckles and asks, "To me? Or in general?"

I scowl at him with my arms crossed. "Both."

Quinn smiles up at me and says, "Sounds good, babe. I'm not looking to get married again, either."

"Okay. Good. I don't want to live together. Ever. Or have kids! I won't ever give your mom grandkids!" I say, with mounting panic.

Another chuckle and another confirmation that we're on the same page.

"I'm serious, Quinnie. I won't ever want to cohabitate."

Quinn sits his guitar down, pulls me into his lap, runs kisses up my neck, and says, "I don't care. I love living alone. I don't want to get married again. I don't want kids. I want you. Well, separate residences, a freezer full of your cooking, and you." He says with a wink as I turn to face him.

I hold his face with our foreheads touching and just breathe his air for a minute.

"Are you sure?" I whisper, both confident and terrified at the answer.

"Absolutely, Sunflower. It's you, me, that damn cat of yours, and our two houses against the world now."

All of the tension drains from my body. This is it. This is my forever.

Chapter 20
Sexy Crocs

Roni

V al cackles when I strut out of my bedroom and down the hall like I'm on a runway in New York.

"Holy shit, Quinn isn't going to know whether to fuck you or laugh at you." They say through their laughter.

"I know, right? He told me we were doing date night in and to wear some sexy lingerie, so here we go!" I say as I do a turn to show off my super tight hot pink crop top that says Sexy Lingerie and black boy shorts with my ass cheeks hanging out with a pair of hot pink and black thigh-high socks. It's sexy, comfortable, and hilarious. I ordered it ages ago and forgot about it until Quinn mentioned "sexy lingerie."

"Okay, Madam Fixing-to-get-Fucked. I'm going to head out so that you can get on with your date night in. What shoes are you wearing?"

"Oh. Damn it." I rack my brain for an idea of where some stripper heels would even be. When was the last time I even wore sexy shoes?

Val chuckles, "Just wear those sexy Crocs of yours, it's not like Quinn will give a shit about your feet with your tits just staring at him like that."

"Yes! Exactly. I can just kick them off on his porch, anyways."

"Coolio, Laters."

I watch Val pull out of the driveway and slide my neon green Crocs on my feet. I mean, it's a look. Not a great one. But still a look. I hustle across the yard and onto his porch, where I kick off the Crocs. And remember that I was bringing the dinner, so back on the Crocs go just as Quinn opens the door and his jaw drops.

"Damn, Sunflower. Just, fuck."

"You like?" I ask as I do a spin and shake the booty for him. The only reply I get is a groan as he grabs me around the waist to pull me against him.

"I love. I love this. I love you. Fuck." He growls just before he slams his mouth against mine. We barely make it into the house before he tosses me over his shoulder and practically runs to his bedroom. I'm tossed on the bed before he covers me with his hard body.

He slowly kisses his way down, stripping my clothes as he does, touching and licking every part of me until he takes my clit into his mouth, sucking and nibbling, his hands sliding up my body to grab my breasts. Rolling my nipples between his large fingers, shooting pleasure straight to my clit, thrusting me into an intense orgasm. Electric wave upon electric wave all over my body. Within the next couple of seconds, his clothes vanish and his thick cock is notched at my entrance. He looks into my eyes as he pushes in, letting me adjust to his size.

Quinn

Her tight warm heat feels like heaven, giving me a pang of worry that I might come too quickly. I hold off, just barely, and pause to gather my wits. No way am I going to blow my load before she gets off again. I slowly pull back, almost completely out of her pussy, before thrusting back in hard. I start a fast pace, one hand grabbing her ass cheek and the other squeezing her nipple. I quickly pull out and flip her over and plunge back into her soaked slit, my heavy balls slapping against her clit. I wrap her hair around my fist and pull her head back while placing open-mouthed kisses up her back. "You got one more for me?" I snarl into her ear as my other hand finds her clit.

"Harder!" she screams as I slap her clit and pound her from behind. Just when I don't think I can go any longer, her pussy squeezes my dick so hard that I have no choice but to follow her into ecstasy.

I collapse on top of her, rolling to the side so I don't crush her too much. I gather her to me to cuddle, but she squeals, "I'm dripping on the bed!" and hops up, cum running down her leg, and rushes into the bathroom. I laugh and look at where she was laying. Sure enough, there is a little puddle. I climb off the bed, take the sheets with me, and toss them in the washer. The shower starts and I hustle back to my woman, getting into the shower right behind her. I slowly slide my hands up her sides, nestling my cock between her ass cheeks. She giggles and slaps my hands away. "I am starving to death. Let me feed you and we'll pick this up afterward."

My stomach growls in response. "I could eat, I guess," I say, chuckling. We quickly bathe and get out. Roni grabs one of my t-shirts that hangs down to her knees, kisses me, and says, "Come help me get our dinner from my house."

"Will do, Sunflower," I say, sliding into a pair of sweats.

We walk hand in hand to Roni's, where we grab the amazing-smelling dishes she packed.

"I wish you had let me cook for you," I said, a wave of guilt tightening my chest because she had to work for our date night.

She laughs, "Absolutely not. You hate to cook, and I love to cook. Why should you do something you hate when I love to do it? Besides, I saw the flowers, candles, and all that when you whisked me off to the bedroom. I love that you put in that much effort."

Feeling pretty darn good about myself, I grab the food from Roni and shoo her into the living room so I can set up the dining room for our date. I set the mason jar of sunflowers and wildflowers in the center on top of the lace tablecloth I borrowed from Momma. After lighting the candles, I plate the steak and potatoes on super fancy breakable plates, which I borrowed from my sister.

Maybe I should invest in some nice shit so I don't have to go on a scavenger hunt to impress my lady.

I flick on the twinkle lights I tacked around the room and dim the rest of the lights. I hear Roni gasp behind me, and I turn to take her in my arms.

"Oh, Quinn, it's beautiful. I love you so much." She murmurs against my chest.

"I love you, too, Sunflower."

Chapter 21

My girlfriend. That's cool as shit.

> Hey babe, leaving work. Want me to come over when I get home? I can grab us some take-out for dinner.

No. I'm in an ill-ass mood so I want to be alone.

> Can I bring you something?

No.

Thanks, though.

> You're welcome

Quinn

I put my phone in the cup holder of my work truck, deciding to run into Walmart and then through the Sonic drive-thru. Roni probably needs some candy. And on her alone days, she tends to nibble instead of cooking.

I walk straight to the candy aisle, snagging a shit-ton, and then up front to grab a couple of cold drinks for my girl. The cashier makes a flirtatious comment about my liking things sweet and I am thrilled to say back, "Nah, but my girlfriend loves these things."

My girlfriend.

That's cool as shit.

Roni

Where did I sit that tea? I wander around the house, picking up my misplaced teacups. None of them are the one that I just made, though. After placing them in the sink, I turn on my electric tea kettle to boil some water. I might as well make a new cup. The old one is probably cold somewhere. While I wait, I put together some salami and an assortment of cheeses on a plate while thinking about what I want to watch on my iPad. I fix up a tea bag and pour the boiling water over it while I try to decide which version of Pride and Prejudice I want to watch. Maybe the zombie one. I pull a little table in front of the papasan, set up the iPad, and put my snack beside it. I think the musical might pull me out of this funk. Or maybe I just need to sleep alone. I have spent the last 4 nights with Quinn beside me, and I love that, but sometimes it's just too much. I'm really quite excited about having a sloth night, where I can just lie down, put snacks on my chest, and shovel them into my mouth while moving super slow. I just wish I had run into town for some candy and maybe a soda or something. Tea and charcuterie seem a little too healthy for sloth night, but what can you do? I've already taken my bra off, so I can't go anywhere.

I find a flavored water in the back of the fridge and bring that with me, and I settle in to start the movie. But before I can even press play, my door opens and Quinn comes strolling in carrying a couple of full grocery bags.

"What the hell, I told you-" I'm cut off as he laughs and dumps the contents of one of the bags into my lap. Oh, this man. It's like 10 bags of assorted gummy candies. My favorites. And from the other bag, he pulls out a can of Arizona tea and a Diet Coke, sits them on the table next to me, and walks out the door. He returns less than a minute later carrying a Sonic bag and a drink. He sits both of them down and leans over to give me a big smacking kiss, grabs my charcuterie board, and walks towards the door, "Thanks for the snack, babe. I'll see you tomorrow." and just walks out the door.

Damn. I adore this man.

Quinn

Chuckling over her irate expression when I walked in, I enter my house. I go straight to the couch and start eating my Sonic dinner and fancy meat and cheese plate while watching an old western on the huge TV that takes up most of the wall. Ah, this feels good. I can't believe it's been a few days since I've been home. Once the movie is over, I pull out my phone and shoot Kenny a text. Maybe we can meet up at the bar. He replies almost instantly with a very enthusiastic *yes* so I push my feet into my boots and head outside. It's been a minute since I've ridden my bike. Damn, the sun and wind feel good on my face.

I pull into Travis's Bar. Luckily, it isn't too packed, and head inside. I know Kenny is already here since I parked my bike next to his, so I look toward the bar for him. Damn it, Bruce is here, too. We've been friends since school, but that asshole rubs me the wrong way. And as if to prove it, before I even get my first beer in my hand, he's already yammering away about shit that doesn't concern him.

"You and Roni have been together for a minute, huh?" asks Bruce as the bartender pushes a couple of beers our way.

"Yup." I smile like I do every time I think of that woman. God, I love her and our life together.

"When are you going to propose? It's about time, ain't it?"

A wave of panic runs over my skin at the thought of us giving up our separate homes and going traditional. It's quickly replaced with a chuckle because could you imagine how my Roni would react to having a 'gross, stinky boy' live with her full-time? She'd kill me within a month.

Damn, that woman is perfect.

"Nah, I'm not going to. Roni and me have a great thing going, and I am not going to wreck that."

"She ain't going to wait around forever, better tie her down before someone else snatches her up," Bruce laughs.

Kenny jumps in, "You don't know Roni. She has no interest in getting married. Period."

Bruce scoffs and roams away. Kenny and I chat about a little of everything for the next hour before he steps outside to call Rhonda. Bruce, seeing another opportunity to bug the shit out of me, walks back over and claps me on the back.

"Dude, like I was saying, a chick's going to expect a proposal. Soon, probably, with y'all's ages and shit. Or you're going to lose her. Kenny doesn't know what he's talking about, him and Rhonda were ready to get married immediately."

I chuckle and say, "Not Roni. That girl has never wanted to live with a man and keeps saying our setup is perfect. Hell, if I sleep over at her house for more than four nights, she tells me it's time for me to take my big ass home."

"Dude, that's exactly what Tiff kept saying, and then the next thing I know, she's married to that douchebag from the casino. I know she left me because I wouldn't marry her. Hell, I thought she didn't want to get married! What chicks say and what they want are two different things."

I laugh then, "Not my Roni. She tells me exactly how it is, especially with living arrangements, and how she absolutely does not want me living with her full-time. And there is no way in hell that she would ever move into what she calls my 'ugly boy house,' but thanks for the concern, bro."

"Look, I'm just trying to help. Do whatever you want, but I've been there."

I roll my eyes. This fucker doesn't know shit.

Kenny comes rushing in, a scowl on his face.

"We should probably head out. Amanda just pulled in. Looks like she is on the prowl."

"Damn it.

My mood dampened, and with work looming at 5 AM tomorrow, I figured I would head home. Get into bed a little early, especially since I've been missing sleep spending nights with my Sunflower.

Not that I'm complaining. Shit, that woman can keep me up every night for the rest of my life.

I sure hope she does.

I pay and turn to go, only to end up with Amanda pressed against me. I gently but firmly push her away and try to walk around her, but she moves to stay in front of me.

"Hey, Quinn," she says, walking her fingers up my chest.

I brush them away, "Amanda. I'm just leaving."

"OK, baby. I'll see you later."

I sigh, trying to hold my temper in check and push past her. Twenty years after our divorce and I still can't shake her.

Chapter 22
Bed-hopping hag strikes again.

Roni

I'm awakened by a car pulling into the driveway. Strange, since neither Quinn nor I usually have visitors at, I look at the clock on the wall: eleven PM. Damn, I missed most of my second movie when I dozed off. I peer out of the window and see a sporty red car coming to a stop in front of Quinn's house and an attractive woman with dark hair and a mini dress gets out and walks straight into Quinn's house as if she owns the place.

My insecurities grip me as my eyes fill up with tears, my vision blurs and the pain in my chest is crippling. Who is she? Did he figure I'd be asleep and not notice? She didn't even try to hide the car. Is she not aware that he is seeing me? Do they want me to see? Sharp pains in my hand have me unfurling my fists, nail marks on my palms.

Get a grip. Quinn would never cheat. There has to be a reasonable explanation.

Right?

Oh, my god.

I haven't known him for that long. He could be that kind of guy.

But I know he isn't.

Wouldn't he cheat in secret?

I should just walk over there and find out. The very idea of catching Quinn cheating freezes me.

He wouldn't.

But she is still in there. She just walked in. He hasn't kicked her out. What business would she have at eleven PM unless she, unless they're...

I can't even think about it.

My chest is caving in. Tears are flowing down my face. I can't breathe.

My thoughts are spiraling.

Of course, he is cheating. Why wouldn't he?

I can't stop staring at his front door, willing him to angrily throw her out. That it was all a mistake. Something. Anything.

I can't move. I can't look away.

I don't know how long I sit here. Sobbing. Spiraling.

After what feels like a lifetime, his front door opens and she walks down the front porch steps. He's in the doorway wearing just pajama pants, no shirt. She turns and runs back up the stairs, throwing herself into his arms.

The room is spinning, the tightness in my chest unbearable. I can't breathe. Oh, god, I can't breathe.

I collapse into the papasan chair, sobbing.

Quinn

I get home from the bar around nine, make myself comfortable in my recliner, and turn on a movie I know Roni would never want to watch. I really want to go over to her house and sleep next to her, but if she doesn't get her alone time, she goes a little crazy.

My god, I love her.

I half doze, half watch the movie, until Roni flings my door open. I grin up at her-Fuck. That's not Roni.

It's my ex-wife, Amanda.

I should have locked my door.

I hope Roni didn't see her arrive.

"What the fuck are you doing here?" I bark, getting up from my recliner.

"Awe, don't be like that, Quinn. I missed you." She purrs, pouting.

"Well, I don't miss you. Now leave. I don't want Roni to see you and get the wrong idea."

Her eyes fill with tears. "Quinn! I just want to talk to you."

Unmoved by her tears, I say, "So talk as I walk you to your car."

"I just missed you so much, baby. And I was hoping..." she trails off with a delicate sniff.

"Hoping what, Amanda?"

"That we could, you know, give us another try. I know we made some mistakes, but we've grown, matured."

"No. Now leave."

She lets the tears slide down her overly made-up cheeks. "Why are you being like this?"

"Because you forced your way into my house and won't leave."

"Just give us another chance. We used to be so good together, you know," she says, stepping towards me.

I step back, "What I know is that you and Derick are getting a divorce and you won't have my alimony to support you."

"That doesn't even matter. Let me stay the night and remind you just how good we are together. I just know you were jealous when I got married. Derick heard you went to the bar that night, drowning your sorrows." She says with a gloating smile.

I laugh cruelly, "I have a gorgeous woman living right next door. Why would I want a bed-hopping hag like you when Roni is right there? The only thing I felt when you got married was relief that I could stop paying for a mistake I made at 18. I was celebrating having my whole paycheck for once in my adult life. Now leave." I snarl as I walk to the door and open it, seeing that Roni's living room lights are on.

Fuck, I have to get over there. I'm so focused on Roni and her thinking the wrong thing that I don't even see it coming when my ex-wife throws her arms around me and kisses me.

I freeze until her tongue thrusts into my mouth, the stale taste of cigarettes snapping me out of my stupor. I shove her away and roar, "Get the fuck off of my property before I call the cops."

"You wouldn't."

"I would. You're trespassing. Leave." I say through clenched teeth.

Amanda glares at me as she leaves, kicking up red dirt as she peels out of the driveway.

I full out run to Roni's house before Amanda's tail lights are even out of view, throwing her door open and finding my love sobbing in the living room. My heart twists in agony. I can't believe I hurt her. I rush over to her and grab her out of the papasan. She pushes me away, crying harder, but I won't let her. I carry her to the bedroom, crawling into the bed with her, reassuring her I would never hurt her.

"Oh, baby. I'm so sorry," I whisper to her.

"Why did you have a woman come over so late?" She asks through her sobs.

"I didn't, Sunflower. I promise. Look at me," I say, lifting her chin to meet my eyes. The tears streaming down her face make my eyes mist. I can't stand this.

"That was my ex-wife. Her and her husband are splitting and she was doing her best to get a new man with some money. She let herself in, and I thought she was you. By the time I realized it wasn't you, she already had the door closed. I told her in no uncertain terms that I was in love with you and would never cheat on you."

"But I saw her kiss you," Roni wails, breaking my heart all over again.

"Yeah, she kissed me. She really caught me off guard, as soon as I opened the door all I could think about was getting to you. Making sure you were ok. And she just threw herself into my arms, as soon as my brain caught up, I threatened to call the cops on her."

"Really?" Roni asks, finally without tears rolling down her face.

"I promise I will never lie to you."

I pull her firmly into my arms, her head on my chest, and we just sit there until her breath stops stuttering. She then mumbles something about needing to wash her face, so I say, "Sit tight. I'll be right back." I give her a kiss on her head and go into her bathroom, grabbing a makeup wipe and her nightly face lotion. She reaches for it, and I hold it out of her reach.

"Please let me."

She gives me a small smile as she nods her head. I gently wipe her face, clearing all the tear tracks and leftover mascara before applying her lotion. Her eyes are still puffy and her nose is red. She is the most beautiful woman I have ever seen. Sitting her lotion and the dirty wipe on the side table, I put my palms on her cheeks and look her in those beautiful eyes. "I love you. Only you. You are the only woman I see. And that will not change until they lay me in the ground. And even then, I will still belong to you."

Her eyes fill with tears, again, but this time she has a small smile on her lovely face. "I knew you wouldn't do that to me, Quinn. But I just..." she trails off, trying to look away.

"Sunflower, I understand."

"I love you, Quinn," she says, leaning in to kiss me, still sniffling.

I kiss her softly, lovingly, until she sighs against my mouth. Then I pepper kisses all over her face, words of love spilling from my mouth, until she falls under me, laughing. I roll us until she is back where she belongs, head on my chest, her hand in mine.

I call out of work the next morning, needing to be there for Roni after such a tumultuous night. I couldn't bear the thought of leaving her bed at 5 AM, and her waking to find me gone. She is so independent and doesn't actually need me, so any time I get the chance to support her, I will take it gladly. I doze for a couple more hours then get up to make Roni breakfast. I hope she stays asleep long enough for me to bring it to her in bed. She can't tolerate anything heavy in the mornings, so I just chop up some fruit and make toast with butter and, of course, a cup of tea.

Food ready, I place it all carefully on a tray and cart it into the bedroom just as Roni is reaching across the bed for me. Christ, I'm glad that I didn't go to work today. Her eyes flick open, filled with sadness, until she spots me, and the sunshine comes out again.

"Hey, there, big boy. Whatcha got?" She murmurs drowsily,

"I made you breakfast in bed, scoot over so I can sit with you."

She moves to the far side of the bed, so I lean over and carefully place the tray over her legs before sliding in beside her. She pats my leg and kisses my cheek. "Thank you, this is wonderful."

"I aim to make every day wonderful," I say, moving just a little closer to her, wanting to feel her against me.

"You do."

We munch in silence, occasionally touching or kissing each other.

When we finish, I get up, grab the tray, and head into the kitchen, Roni following behind me.

"I want to spend the day with you, but then we have to sleep separately. Is that okay?" Roni says nervously.

"Of course, that's okay. I figured that was how it was going to be since you didn't get your full night last night and all the emotional junk. Damn, babe, I am so sorry about last night."

"Hey, it's alright. I am not upset with you, like, at all."

"You should be, it's my fault you were hurt," I say, rubbing her thigh.

"Did you invite her over?"

"Of course not!"

"Then it's not your fault. It's hers. Just next time, call me if she shows up. I want to take a whack at her," Roni says with a smirk.

My chuckle grows into a full bellied laugh, "Oh, I would love to see that!"

"I would love to do it!"

Chapter 23
Quinn's hoe-bag of an ex-wife

Roni

I pull into Val's driveway, laying on the horn. They hustle outside, not expecting me, and I yell, "Get in loser, we're going shopping! Also, I have gossip."

"Gossip about who?" They ask, walking up and leaning in the window.

"Me, Quinn, and his ex-wife."

"I'm in. Let me go throw on some clothes," Val says, turning to run inside. I roam over to the backyard to talk to Memaw for a bit. I just love Val's cantankerous grandmother.

She looks up at me from her lawn chair and says, "Roni. Married that large man you caught yet?"

I laugh, "Absolutely not."

"Good girl. Men will ruin your life."

Our conversation over, we sit in companionable silence until Val barrels out the back door. Wearing hot pink wide-leg pants with a lime green tank top, their platinum hair in disarray, and their makeup perfect, they squeal, "Let's go! I need a little drinky before the gossip."

I hop up and bid Memaw farewell, and away we go.

Three sexy pairs of shoes, two hours and one coffee later, Val and I are roaming aimlessly through the mall, window shopping and chatting.

"Oh! The gossip!"

"What gossip?" Val asks.

"Quinn's fucking hoe-bag of an ex-wife."

"Oh, shit. What happened?"

"So, I was doing a sloth night, right? I dozed off and woke up in the middle of the night to a car pulling into the driveway. It was some bitch in a club outfit walking right into Quinn's house."

"What the fuck? Are we going to murder Quinn?"

A laugh bursts from me, "No, no. Quinn is fine. Poor guy was snoozing in the recliner when she barged in, begging for my damn man."

"Did you run over there with a rolling pin?"

I make a disgusted sound. "I wish. Instead, I just sobbed in my living room until Quinn ran over to explain everything."

"And you believe him?"

"Yeah, at the very least, he's smart enough to not cheat on me in a house that I can see from my house."

"True that. Is she hotter than you?"

"Oh, um. I don't think so. Maybe opposite hot? I don't know; she's a super tight clothing with make-up layered on, kind of hot. I'd see the appeal if she wasn't such a bitch."

"Holy cow, speaking of hot, look at that set!" Val says, pointing to a hot pink babydoll nightie displayed in the window of Lenora's Lingerie.

"Dibs!" I call speed walking toward the store.

"Why I oughta," Val says in a 1950s sitcom voice, shaking their fist at me.

Laughing, I snag a nightie in my size while Val grabs one in lime green. I scowl at them, but they just shrug. "You called dibs on the pink one. Besides, I won't be fucking Quinn, so who is going to know we have the same sexy clothes?"

"I'll know," I say, smirking.

"Well, if you are thinking of me while wearing that, either you and I need to have a serious conversation or Quinn needs to step up his game."

Quinn

My clock says 12:47 a.m., but that can't be right. Who would call me at 12:47 a.m. on a Thursday night when everyone knows I have to work in the morning? It had better be an emergency.

I answer the phone without even looking at the caller ID and growl out, "Do you know what fucking time it is?" Only to hear a soft gasp at my harsh words, and then my Sunflower says, "Oh, I'm so sorry. I didn't even look at the time before I called. I'm so sorry, Quinnie, go back to sleep." then the line goes dead as my chest fills with ice. She's the only one that can call me whenever she wants and I just hurt her feelings. I have to apologize. Right now. I hop out of bed and throw on some pajama pants and my pink Crocs, not bothering with a shirt. I half jog over to her door and start laying on the doorbell. I will not let her ignore me. As soon as she opens the door, her gorgeous eyes watery, I barrel into her and wrap her in a huge bear hug.

"Not you, Sunflower. Never you. You can call me anytime. And I might growl, but I'm never growling at you. You just tell me to shut up. Ok?"

She gives a congested laugh and says, "I know this. I do." She sighs and continues, "I just had this whole bit planned out and I didn't even realize you would be asleep, didn't even realize the time, and then you were so mean."

"Bit? What bit?"

"Well, I got new lingerie..." she says, trailing off on the last word.

"And?" I ask excitedly, every bit of blood rushing to my cock.

"I thought you might like to see it, " she said, stepping back and removing her robe to reveal a hot pink lacy babydoll nightie.

Jesus Christ.

"Fuck, yes," I say against her mouth as I yanked her to me. My hands travel down the soft lace to grab her ample ass, and I barely contain my groan. That ass is perfection. I maneuver her against the front door and press my entire hard body against her soft one, just feeling her for a minute before I capture her lips. Picking her up, she wraps her legs around my waist, and I walk us inside, tossing her on the bed.

I crawl over her, whispering apologies to every body part, this magnificent woman that I keep accidentally hurting. I vow that I would never intentionally hurt her. I slowly graze my fingertips over her, causing goosebumps to break out over her legs, then hips, stomach, around her luscious lace-covered breast, all the way up to cup her cheeks, "I love you." I breathe into her mouth before ravaging it. My hands leave her face to circle her nipples, feeling them pebble beneath my thumbs. She moans softly, making me so hard I can barely stand it. Slowly, I work my way back down her body, gently touching over the lace, listening to her whimper. I pull the lacy g-string down her legs, blowing on her clit as I do so. One lick and I can't restrain myself. I ravenously feast on her pussy, reveling in her moans, sliding my finger inside of her until I feel her thighs clamp, trembling, around my head.

"Quinn!" she yells as she comes. I keep going until she pushes me away. I wipe my mouth on the back of my hand, rip off my pajama pants, and crawl up her fantastic body, kissing, licking and grabbing. Gently, slowly, I push into her heat, groaning, listening to her whimper, and beg for more. Setting a leisurely pace, I press my thumb to her clit. With slow circles and slow thrusts, I keep her right on the edge until she moans, "Quinn, please. I need more."

I slam into her, making her gasp, and growl, "Then more is what you'll get."

I let go, shoving into her harshly, pressing her clit in fast circles until I feel her pussy ripple and she comes with a shout. I follow immediately after, collapsing onto her, whispering my love until we both stop trembling.

Roni

The next morning, I find myself trapped under Quinn's large body, a cocoon of warmth and love. But also lying in a sticky mess of cum.

I tickle Quinn's side, making him jerk awake with a groan.

"It's too early, Sunflower, let's sleep in a little bit."

"I can't. I'm covered in cum. It's sticky. And you have to leave for work in like 45 minutes."

"Oh, shit." He laughs, climbing off of me and pulling me up.

We brush our teeth while the shower heats up and then step into the shower. We managed to get all cleaned up with only a little bit of funny business.

"Alright, babe, will I see you tonight?" Quinn asks, putting his shoes on.

"Maybe at bedtime, Val is coming over."

He wiggles his eyebrows at me. "Sounds good. You can crawl into my bed anytime."

"Oh, hush, you goose," I say, standing up to give him a kiss before he rushes out the door.

"Love you!" He yells as he climbs into his truck.

I yell it back and blow him an exaggerated kiss, that he catches and holds to his heart. It's all I can do to keep myself from chasing down his truck as it pulls out of the driveway, just to kiss him one more time.

Chapter 24
Fighting off attackers in undies.

Roni

"I'm, like, really, really in love with him. Like my soul might die without him." I say, laying on my amethyst velvet sofa, my head on a teal pillow. Val is lying on my faded rug, reading a battered romance novel that they promptly dog ear while sitting up.

"Of course you do. I knew from the moment I met him that you two were endgame."

"No, you did not. I just figured it out, like a month ago."

Val rolls their eyes and says, "It really takes you a while to figure out shit. But either way, hurray for finally falling in love!"

"I don't know. If we don't work out, that would be one of the worst things to happen to me, I think. Like dead parents and then Quinn leaving."

"Ver-Ver and Quinny sitting in a tree, K-I-S-S-I-N-G, first comes love-" Val abruptly stops singing when the pillow I throw hits them in the face.

"I'm trying to be serious," I say with a huff once I stop giggling.

"No, you are trying to be stupid and panic over a good thing."

"I am not!"

"Look, Quinn is a solid guy. He obviously adores you. Unless you dump him or cheat on him or something, I don't see that fellow going anywhere."

"Really?" I ask, heart pounding.

"Duh, you know I wouldn't defend a gross, stinky boy if I could help it. But Quinn really does seem to be the best of the stinky boys."

"He really is, isn't he?"

"Yup. Now that we have figured out your love life, let's do something fun."

"Well, I have an idea..."

Quinn

The opening strands of that new super girly pop album play, a squeal, and the shattering of glass filter in over the sound of my guitar. What the fuck? I rush out my door, running towards Roni's house, certain I will have to fight off a burglar in my boxers and bare feet in the rain. Then the giggles start.

I peer around the corner of her house and see...

Well, I'm not exactly sure what is going on.

Roni and Val are twirling in the rain, each holding a mason jar of a pinkish liquid that they are sipping through straws. The music is cranked up, and their movements would be almost ritualistic if they stopped giggling so much.

"I don't think we're doing it right." Val gasps over the song, the drink sloshing onto their hand.

"This is exactly what the book says we should do," Roni says, gesturing to the covered porch and chugging her drink.

"Did the book also say to get wine drunk and then do it? In the rain?"

"Kind of." Roni snort-laughs. "It said to be comfortable and secure in your magic. Wine makes me comfortable and secure in my magic. So it basically told me to get sloshed."

"Damn. It really did. I hope this gives you the harvest you wanted and we aren't summoning a demon or something stupid."

"Could we summon a demon? That'd be one hell of a conversation starter. 'Nice to meet you, Mrs. Smith. Have you met my demon named Dan?' Could you imagine?" Roni practically chortles the last sentence out.

"No, dummy, the demon would eat your face."

"Party pooper."

"Because I won't let a demon eat your face?"

"Yes, you get it."

"Fine. Get eaten. See if I care. Are we going to finish this or not? I think my wine is more rainwater than alcohol by now." Val says as they glare at Roni and take a sip of what is definitely a good bit of rainwater and wine.

"Yes, yes. Let's start over and see what shakes out."

"A fucking goblin is what is going to shake out. A fucking goblin."

"I thought it was going to be a demon..."

I lean against the side of the house. I should give them privacy, but this show is just too good. The dancing starts again, Roni with her wild hair plastered to her face by the rain, a cropped mustard yellow top, and a long flowy emerald green skirt soaking wet and wrapping around her legs, her face upturned to the sky as the rain drizzles down. Roni's arms are around Val, laughing up into the rain. Val's neon green sports bra and athletic booty shorts starkly contrast my Roni's earth goddess vibe, but they are perfect together. I should go home and let them have this time together. But I can't resist inserting myself into their orbit. Hoping they like me enough to let me stay. I know Roni loves me, but I also know that Val will always be the most important person in Roni's life. I might be the love story, the happily ever after, but they are the soulmates.

"Is this a private dance party or can anyone join?" I ask once the current song ends.

Val squeals and throws their mason jar at my head as Roni freezes, staring at me in shock. Luckily, Val is tipsy and has horrible aim, and the jar lands in the grass yards away from me.

"Quinnie-boy!" Roni squeals as she skip-dances towards me. I open my arms and wait for her to slam into me, then I spin her in a circle as her magical giggle surrounds me. For a moment, it's just us in this gentle rainstorm.

A moment that is quickly shattered.

"Why are you naked?" Val screams, "My eyes! Won't someone think of the children!"

"What children?" I ask with a chuckle.

"Me!" Val shrieks, "I'm children!"

Laughing, I ask, "What was that glass smashing? I thought someone was breaking in over here, hence the boxers."

"Awe, you were going to fight off attackers in your undies!" Val says while Roni is saying, "Oh! We dropped a bottle of wine and didn't want to cut ourselves, so we barricaded it until we're more sober."

I kiss her temple and flick Val's nose as I head towards my house, "Y'all carry on. I'm going to put on pants and then clean up the glass. I don't want y'all cut."

"Thank you, Sugar-Bear!" Roni says, tugging me back in for another kiss. I smile against her lips and tell her, "I kind of like that one."

That magical giggle wraps itself so tightly around my heart that it almost hurts.

I make my way back to my house, throw on yesterday's jeans, and grab my broom, dustpan, and a grocery bag. Back in the drizzle, I sweep up the glass, tossing it in the bag and then in the big trash can. Afterward, I head back to Roni and Val to give Roni a kiss and leave them be, but Roni pulls me into her arms and starts to sway slowly. My heart pounding, I kiss her forehead and say, "I don't want to interrupt, just wanted to give you a kiss before heading back inside."

"You can stay. I just texted my ride. He'll be here in a couple of minutes," Val inserts.

"He?" I ask, wiggling my eyebrows.

"Yes, he. The man that works for my Memaw. We've got a meeting in the morning, so he promised to pick me up if we drank tonight. We drank, and he's picking me up. Nothing else to say."

"Mighty defensive," I say, and Val scowls at me and stomps away.

Roni giggles and puts her head on my chest. I don't know how long we stay like this, but it feels like forever—and yet, it's not long enough. We hear a car in the driveway as Val runs towards us.

"My ride's here," Val says, pulling Roni to them for a hug. Then they look me up and down, scowling, before hugging me and running around the corner. I chuckle, pulling Roni back into my chest, and we continue to sway to the music.

After a few minutes, Roni reaches up, wraps a hand around the back of my neck, and pulls me down for a magical kiss.

Smiling against my lips, she says, "I love you."

"I love you, too, Sunflower."

"Good. Now go home."

I laugh, "Yes, ma'am. Just give me one, maybe two, more magical kisses, and I think I can survive."

Giggling, she does just that.

Chapter 25

Put some pants on.

Quinn

"Roni! Put some pants on!" I bellow as I stomp through her front door.

"Why?" she asks as she walks out of her kitchen, teacup in hand.

"Because I said so, woman. You do as I say." I growl against her mouth as I pull her against me.

That magical giggle again. Oh, my heart.

"Or I could sit down and drink my tea and read a book without pants on." She says snarkily.

"Now come on, I wanna go for a ride. Put some pants and boots on!"

"You could have said something instead of practically grunting like a caveman." She laughs, sitting her tea down on a stack of books, and heads towards her bedroom, with me prowling behind her. She thinks I'm a caveman, huh? I reach out, grab her arm, and spin her around before tossing her over my shoulder. She squeals and giggles as I walk into her room and toss her on the bed. Immediately after, I cover her soft body with my hard, very hard, body.

"You know what," I say in between kissing her sweet mouth, "We could go for a ride another day. Maybe we just stay here. Hmm?"

She laughs, pushing against my chest, "Oh, no, we are not! You barged in my door, making demands. You aren't changing the plan now."

"Anything for you, Sunflower," I say with a sigh as I get up. I reach down to help her up and then slap her ass. She yelps and glares at me as she walks over to her closet to get dressed for a ride. I sit on her bed to watch the show.

She covers those gorgeous legs with a pair of skin-tight jeans, holy hell, and pulls on her Docs before tossing a lightweight jacket over her t-shirt. She grins at me as she braids her hair and says, "Where are we riding to?"

I answer, "Out to the pier to watch the sunset over the water."

"Oh, Quinnie! That sounds lovely!" She says, dancing up to kiss me. I grab her around the waist and pull her onto my lap. She giggles and tries to pull away but I don't let her.

"Just a couple more kisses, babe, then I think I can make it."

Another magical giggle, and another couple of magical kisses, then off we go.

The ride is amazing. It always is with Roni wrapped around me, and the wind on my face. We get to the little beach and find a parking spot about 20 minutes before the sun sets; there is plenty of time to find a spot. Roni's hand fits perfectly in mine as we make our way towards the picnic tables and play equipment. Sunflower drags me over to the swings and settles herself on one. I choose to push her rather than let my big ass break one of these flimsy-looking things. She pumps her legs to get higher and higher, and even though I know she's a grown woman and not in actual danger, my heart doesn't like her so high off the ground. But I keep that thought to myself. Roni would never let me live it down if I panicked over her on a child's swing set.

Then she jumps.

One moment she's safe enough on the swing, the next she is flying through the air and then landing on her butt in the sand.

"Sunflower!" I squeak before hearing her snort-laugh and knowing she's just fine. I stomp over to her and throw her over my shoulder, slapping her ass and telling her she isn't to do that ever again.

Her magical giggle follows us to a picnic table, where I gently sit her on the top. I climb up next to her and grab her hand just as the sky turns pink and orange. The love of my life leans over and rests her head on my shoulder.

"This is just perfect, Sugar-bear." She sighs.

I wrap my arms around her, pulling her into my lap, trying to get as close as possible without having the cops called on us.

"Yes, it is, Sunflower."

Roni

I let myself into Quinn's house, finding him sitting in his recliner eating a bowl of cereal. He smiles at me around a mouth full of Lucky Charms, "What's up, Sunflower?"

"Your sisters and I are going to the flea market this morning. Wanna come with?"

"Are Chris and Donny going?"

"Yup."

"Alright, I'm in. When do you want to leave?"

"As soon as you're ready."

"Alright, babe, let me finish my cereal and put my shoes on, and we'll head out. Meeting them there, right?"

"Yes, can we take your bike?" I ask, already excited.

"Of course."

The ride is magnificent. It's a beautiful sunny day, warm but not hot. Perfect for walking around the flea market, with a big lemonade and some boiled peanuts. We lost the guys at a stretch of booths selling tools, guitars, and sports equipment, but there was no way we were going to stand around when we had all these cool things to plunder through.

I haven't gotten the chance to chat with Quinn's sisters in a minute, so I catch them up on the ex-wife drama. "Let me tell you, seeing her just let herself into Quinn's house just broke my heart. I always thought I'd be the baseball bat to the kneecaps kind of gal, but instead, I'm a sobbing heap lady."

"I bet if you see her again, you'd be the baseball bat to the kneecaps kind of girl," says Amber, laughing.

"Nah, if Amanda is dumb enough to go back over to Quinn's, I think Roni would be a never-find-the-body kind of woman."

We laugh, and I say, "I don't know. As much as I'd like to see her dumped in the bayou for gater food, I also don't look great in orange. And the ex-husband's girlfriend is always at the top of the suspect list."

"Well, if she disappears, it couldn't happen to a better woman. I was just a kid when she and Quinn split, but I remember how horrible she was. She was always mean to Amber and me, telling us if we told Quinn that she was treating us that way, that he wouldn't believe us and we'd never see him again. I was terrified she was going to take him away from us," Nicole says as we turn a corner and I see her, Amanda, laughing with a group of women. I grab Amber's arm and yank her back around the opposite side, Nicole following.

"Fuck, fuck, fuck." I say, almost panicking.

"What is it?" Amber asks, looking around for the source of my panic.

"I just saw Amanda."

"Speak of the devil and she shall appear," Amber says, rolling her eyes. "I forgot she ran her momma's booth up here."

"Let's just skip this row. I don't want any drama today." I say with a sinking feeling.

"We aren't letting some home-wrecker chase us away!" Nicole says, outraged.

"I'm just still feeling raw about that night. I don't think I can see her face to face."

"You don't think Quinn invited her or anything like that, do you?"

"No! Of course not. I know he's loyal, it's just... it was a really hard night."

"Don't worry, Roni, I got this," Nicole assures me before storming around the corner towards the group of women. Amber reaches out and grabs her arm, but Nicole just shakes her off and keeps going.

With nothing left to do, Amber and I peer around the corner and watch Nicole walk right up to Amanda, punch her in the nose like she's defending herself against a shark, and takes off running towards us.

"Come on!" she says with a playful huff as she rushes over to us. "Let's hurry and get out of here before they decide to call security on us!"

Damn it, she's right. We start power-walking through the crowd until we spot the guys. We don't even stop, just kind of jog past them yelling, "Come on, we have to leave. Now!"

The boys look baffled but drop whatever they're looking at and run with us.

We get to the parking lot, and the men have questions.

"What the hell, Amber? You made me come all this way for an hour?" Donny asks, throwing his hands up. All the men nod in agreement and make little comments like "Yeah, what gives?" and "Why were y'all running anyway?"

The three of us look at each other and just crack up. We know we should leave, but the boys aren't going anywhere until we explain, and we can't explain until we stop laughing. Finally, catching our breath—no easy feat considering the running and laughing—I look at Quinn and say, "So, what happened was Nicole kind of punched Amanda in the face, and now we should probably leave before the cops show up."

"Holy shit, that is so hot. I wish I could have seen it." Nicole's husband, Chris, says, pulling her to him. She giggles and shrugs, "Maybe next time," as Chris grins down at her.

Donny says, "Well, I guess we should head on then. Not trying to bail my wife out of jail today, gotta pick up the kids in a couple of hours. Let's try this again when the ladies aren't so violent."

Laughing, we all say goodbye, and then it's just Quinn and me on the back of his bike, flying down the scenic route home.

The rest of the day is spent in bed, feeding each other, fucking, and retelling Quinn the story of his ex-wife getting punched in the face over and over again.

Chapter 26
Sliding out of the bathtub like seals.

> Whatcha up to today?

Just working. I have 3 projects to finish up and another to start. Val's laptop finally came in, so they'll probably show up later.

> They work with you?

Nah, they're a graphic artist but when we're in the same town, we usually meet up and do our work in the same space. We like to pretend that we are working in an office.

> Will I see you later? Or are you heading out before I get off?

Oooh. I dunno. I'll text you this afternoon and let you know.

Okay, either way, I've got a tater tot casserole in my freezer just calling my name.

Lucky you.

Very.

Roni

"Look at it!" Val practically screams at me, "Isn't it the prettiest laptop you've ever seen?" They hold up their new laptop, which has been customized with a turquoise sticker cover with pink stripes. It's both obnoxious and so perfect that I laugh.

"I mean, for you? Yeah." I say, still laughing.

"Obviously, you wouldn't tote this beast around. You would look ridiculous. Anyways. Guess what I've named him? You'll never guess. Drum roll, please! Hims name is FUCK-" Val is cut off as Ginger takes a swipe at their neck from the back of the sofa. "You miserable beast of burden!"

I clamp my lips together, doing my best to swallow the laughter bubbling up, as I reach for my feline companion and remove her from the situation. A mournful basset hound watches me from the kitchen, clearly displeased by Ginger's antics.

"I know you're trying not to laugh, Veronica Fuckface Corbin!" Val shrieks at me.

"How'd you know my middle name?" I cackle as I settle myself in the papasan by the window.

"Shut up." Val rolls their eyes at me and starts pulling out their work junk.

The hours fly by as we get our work done together separately. I'm completely absorbed in the story that I'm editing when I hear Val say, "Ugh, I gotta charge my tampon, but I don't want to get up."

My thoughts stutter to a stop as I'm fully pulled into the moment. "What the actual hell?" I ask with an incredulous laugh.

Val fumbles with their laptop and gives me a blank look, followed by "Huh?"

"Why do you need to charge a tampon?" I ask, still unable to grasp this conversation.

"I don't..." They trail off, rubbing at their eyebrows before they laugh uncontrollably. "Tammel!" They gasp as a sneaky tear trails down their flushed cheek.

Frustration builds in my chest as I bark out, "What?"

Still laughing but no longer hysterical, Val says, "I named my laptop Tammel. I said I need to charge Tammel!"

Jesus Christ on a cranberry cracker.

Of course, they did.

We call it a day and Val says, "Lookie what I brought."

I'm stuck in the damn papasan, trying not to upturn it as I climb out, but I glance over to see that Val is holding up a bottle of champagne with a big grin on their face.

"Mimosas! Let's grab some snacks and the orange juice and sit out on the back porch."

Val raids the pantry for their preferred salty snacks while I dig through my basket of sour candies that Quinn keeps stocked for me. We load up a basket with our goodies and juice and head out back. We've finished the bottle and are feeling tipsy when Val asks, "So, how big is Quinn's dick?"

I inhale a gummy bear and start coughing, "Christ on a cracker, warn a bitch before just coming right out with the big questions."

"Oh, big, huh? Like big, big, or like, it's big enough?" Val asks, finishing the last of their drink.

"You know I don't ride and confide."

"Since when?"

"Since I decided I wanted to keep this one. Not in my house, of course, but in his house."

"Fine. Wanna see my wedding Pinterest board?"

"Wedding?" I practically yell, "Since when are you having a wedding?"

"I'm not." Val cackles, "I just like planning one on Pinterest. It's all the fun and none of the whole having a husband bullshit."

"Ooh, I wanna!" I say, hopping up to go grab my iPad. When I get back and sit down, Val snatches it from me and logs into their account. They spend the next half hour taking me through their imaginary wedding, and then we plan mine.

"Quinn would shit himself if he walked in on us planning my wedding," I say, still giggly from the mimosas.

"I think he'd marry you, though. He seems all in."

"He doesn't want to get married any more than I do. Said he's been there and done that."

"But if you wanted to."

"Yes, I'm sure he would do it for me if I wanted to. He really is a sweet man, isn't he? If I ever were to get married, I'd want it to be him."

"Wow, that was super mushy. We need more booze if you're getting all romantic and shit. Do you have any?"

"No," I whine, "Wait! I bet Quinn does! Let's go raid his stash."

"Ooh, I like you with a boyfriend," Val says in a mock teasing tone while making kiss noises.

"Oh, shush. Now, do you want my boyfriend's booze or not?"

"Of course, I want his booze. Let's go plunder!"

We make our way across the yard, where I stoop down to pull Quinn's spare key from under his mat, and we let ourselves in.

"Ewe, pretty sparse, isn't it?" Val says, taking in Quinn's mostly blank walls, his old brown sofa, and his snazzy gray recliner. His house is bare, with four guitars on the far wall and a couple of large framed photos of lakes and mountains his sisters brought over. A large record collection and record player take up the space under the window. He promised I could bring over all the macrame pieces I desired, so he has three hanging plants in their macrame hangers in front of the window. And that's about it for decor.

"It is rather dull, isn't it? And he loves it this way. The only reason he has the photos up is because he didn't want to hurt his sisters' feelings. They did as much decorating as he would let them."

"I see why you guys can't live together. He'd go crazy in your maxed-out maximalist house."

I crack up, "I know, right?" as I open the cabinet over his refrigerator, snagging his Crown Royal.

"This is all he has," I said, holding up the bottle. Val makes a disgusted face and says, "Boys are so gross."

"Hey!"

"Yeah, yeah. Fine. Do you have coke? I can drink it with coke."

I look in his fridge. "I don't, but Quinn has a couple of different cokes. What do you want? Coke? Not root beer or Dr. Pepper, right?"

"Yeah, Coke in that nasty shit."

"Coke it is," I say as I pour us a drink. I love whisky; it's about all I drink, but Val's facial expressions while drinking it make it even better. We decide to stay at Quinn's house since he has the booze and sodas, and we don't want to carry shit to my house.

An hour and a finished bottle of Crown later, we are pretty shit-faced and giggly.

Val gets up, declaring, "I want some sweet tea," and proceeds to drop the pitcher immediately as soon as it's in their hands. All over the inside of the refrigerator and all over the floor.

"Fuck!" They screech and throw the whole roll of paper towels in the puddle.

I'm laughing so hard that I almost pee all over myself and stagger to the bathroom. Val wanders in, saying, "I'm sticky. Let's take a bath."

"Yes! Oh, I love drunk baths!"

"Me too!"

We strip down to our underwear while the tub fills with water and carefully get in, sitting with our butts in the water and our legs over the side.

"I wish we had music," Val says mournfully.

"Oh! I'll go turn on the record player. Sweet, sweet Sugar-Bear made sure I had music here."

"That's a nice boy you found," Val says as I try to figure out how to get my drunk ass out of the slippery tub without breaking my neck. We have a quick discussion and decide to get out like seals. Just slide over the edge to land on our hands and then knees on dry land.

We do so without dying.

I don't see towels and can't remember where Quinn keeps them, so I crawl down the hall and toward the living room.

Val, on the other hand, declares, "Crawling is for losers, I shall roll!" and promptly rolls right out of the bathroom door and into the hall wall. They just lay there, upside down, glaring at me as I laugh.

We make our way to the living room, leaving a trail of water that we swear we will clean up as soon as we start playing the tunes.

Which is easier said than done. How the hell does he have his records organized? We can't find any good ones, even though we've taken just about all of them off the shelf. Oh! Over there, on the side table, are a couple of records I like. We pick one and figure out the record player. Luckily, I've seen Quinn do it a billion times, so I kind of know how.

"Our water is going to get cold. We can just clean this up later," Val says, butt-scooting towards the bathroom. I manage to make it to my feet and follow them.

Quinn

I'm a little worried on the drive home. Roni told me she'd text me and let me know her plans for the evening, but she never did. I texted her and even called once and she didn't reply, which is totally unlike her. I know she's with Val, so she's probably fine, but I need to make sure. The job ran over today, which only adds to my stress since I'm about two hours late getting home. I pull into the driveway, relieved to see Roni's Jeep and Val's Subaru. I hop out without a glance at my house and head straight to Roni's. Opening the door, I'm greeted with a howl from a very disgruntled Basset hound and no Roni. I walk through the house, more befuddled as I go. Ginger winds herself through my legs, almost tripping me, until I pick her up. And then she promptly bites my arm. Of course, little asshole. Where the hell are they? I walk out to the back porch and see an empty champagne bottle, sticky mason jars, empty candy wrappers, and Roni's iPad. But no Roni or Val. I pick up Roni's tablet, punching in the code to see if they left a damn clue of their whereabouts. It opens to a fully planned wedding Pinterest board. Strange, that's Roni's account. Do we know someone getting married? I shake off the scarier thoughts of Roni planning her own wedding and continue my hunt for my lady and her bestie. I don't know why they'd be at my house but it's the last place to check before I start searching the woods. Halfway there, I hear one of those chick bands I bought for Roni; thank goodness, they must have wanted to check out the records. I notice my front door is cracked, which is strange, so I just push it open.

What the hell happened here?

A trail of water leads from the record player down the hall, hopefully to the bathroom. My records are scattered across the floor, almost as if someone just dumped them out. My pitcher of sweet tea and a soggy roll of paper towels are on the kitchen floor.

And Roni's magical giggle is coming from down the hall.

Worried about what I'll find down the hall but eager to see Roni's smiling face, I follow the sounds of splashing water and laughter—and the actual trail of water—all the way to my bathroom. Roni and Val are in the tub, splashing each other and laughing. My heart stutters to see her so happy, and I don't want to interrupt, but I have questions that need answering and a mess to clean up.

They haven't noticed me, so I decide to give them a few more minutes before I bring the thunder and go clean up their mess. I find my empty bottle of Crown and Coke cans littering the floor around the trash can. Well, that explains it, I chuckle to myself. They'll be feeling it tomorrow. I throw a couple of fluffy towels in the dryer and walk over to Roni's house to grab some clothes for them, then I feed the pets since it's almost dinnertime. Back at my house, the splashing, giggles, and chick tunes serenading me, I clean up my girl and her person's mess. Then I grab the towels and go to the bathroom,

"Okay, kids, time to get out of the bath."

They both startle, look at me, and then without even the decency to look guilty, they both start laughing again.

As Roni snort-laughs, I reach down to pull her up, but she says "No! Wait! We figured out how to get out on our own. Back up!"

So I do and watch my almost 40-year-old girlfriend and her best friend drunkenly slide out of my bathtub like seals.

I think I fall in love all over again, my life will never be boring with this sparkling woman in my life.

I help them to their feet and wrap them both in the warm towels, sending them down the hall to my bedroom where their clothes await.

"Hey," I holler down the hall, "Y'all want me to run into town and grab Waffle House?"

"Waffle House!" They both yell gleefully, so I grab my keys and tell them I'll be back in a few minutes.

"No, no, Sugar-Bear, we want to go! We've been stuck in the house all day! We want to be where the people are!" And from there Val joins in as they sing that song from the mermaid movie.

Knowing that they forgot about me for a minute, I head outside, resigned to taking two drunks to Waffle House at 7 in the evening, and lock Roni's house up after checking that the pets are still cool. Outside, Roni and Val are sitting on my porch, eyes squinting, trying to help each other tie their shoes. I crack up and jog over there to help.

Luckily, by the time we get to the Waffle House, the lushes are sleepy and giggly, much less likely to cause a scene. I walk in with Roni under one arm and Val holding my hand. I lead them to the booth in the back and get them seated on the same side of the booth, snuggled up together. Dora chuckles as she walks over. "Well, what do we have here?"

"Roni and Val did a little day drinking and somehow we ended up here."

"Where else would they allow a couple drunk gals and a large man at this early hour?" Dora laughs.

"Yes, ma'am, you are right about that," I say with a chuckle.

"Oh Dora, Quinn almost married you, you know?" Roni says out of nowhere and to my horror.

"Well, uh, I, you see-" I start as Dora laughs.

"Oh, hell, no," She says, again to my horror.

"What's wrong with marrying me?" I exclaim to Dora, laughing even harder with Roni and Val joining in.

"Son, I've been married and divorced twice. No way in hell I'm trying that again," Dora says as she walks away with our drink order. She comes back a few minutes later, sitting our sweet teas and coffee in front of us.

"What's your favorite thing on the menu?" Val asks Dora, slurring their words together.

"I'm quite partial to a cheeseburger and hash browns, smothered and covered," Dora answered, smirking.

"Oh, that sounds good. I'll take that." Roni says at the same time Val says, "I'll take one!"

I chuckle. "Well, I might as well make it easy on you. Three cheese-burgers with hash browns smothered and covered."

"Alright, baby, I'll be back with y'alls order just as soon as it's done."

Roni and Val talk about the jukebox and what song they should play, but before they can coerce my quarters off me, Dora shows up with our grub. Luckily, they are drowsy enough to sort of giggle and eat and whisper until I have to carry both of them out to the truck.

Once I get them home, I lay Val on the sofa with a glass of water and a bottle of Tylenol on the table next to them, and I try to pull their shoes off. They swat at me and almost kick me in the face before falling back to sleep. Then I pull their stupid shoes off. The shoes they struggled so much to tie, but have a zipper on the sides.

Seems about right.

Roni manages to walk in and sits on the floor, snuggling Ginger and trying to keep her eyes open. After I lock down the house and arrange the pets, I pick up Roni and carry her to bed.

As soon as I have her in my arms, she snuggles into me, kissing my neck, and nibbling on my ear. I chuckle, digging this cuddly and horny version of my lady. I toss her onto the bed, making her giggle, before taking her shoes off and tugging her leggings down her legs. She hadn't put on panties before leaving so I have an excellent view of her bare pussy. I could just stare at this woman all night.

Instead, I tickle her foot, needing to hear her laughter again. She snatches her foot away and sits up, slowly crawling towards me. When she is at eye level with my crotch, she reaches out and tries to unbuckle my pants, whining when her uncoordinated fingers can't get it unbuckled. Smiling, I help her, opening my pants for whatever she wants to do to me. She yanks my pants and boxers down, leans over, licks the tip, giggles, and falls backward on the bed. I chuckle, thinking she's out for the night, before hearing her slur out, "Fuck my face, Sugar-Bear." I push my pants off and crawl over her body, finding her mouth in an O shape, waiting for my dick to fill it. I can't help the laugh that escapes. Luckily, she cracks up, too.

I pull my shirt over my head and then pull her's off, both of us still chortling, and I climb into bed next to her. She's so cuddly, her hands roaming my body, giggling. I squeeze her to me as her movements slow. Moments later her breathing evens out.

I smile, holding her close as sleep overtakes me.

Chapter 27
Or whatever Mr. Darcy said.

Quinn

I slowly wake up and roll over to pull Roni back into my arms where she belongs, only to find a cold, empty bed. I can not believe Roni is up this early after getting trashed with Val last night, but good for her. I throw on a pair of joggers and my t-shirt from the floor and head towards the living room to kiss my girl. When I hear giggles from the sunroom, I turn that way, intent to eavesdrop, and what I hear almost kills me.

"Ewe, a baby?" Val asks incredulously.

Roni giggles and says, "Yes. I want a squishy one. With like 3 rolls on each leg and a triple chin. I want to sit in that chair over there, nap, and cuddle with a fat little roly-poly."

Val bursts into laughter and fuck, I get it. I feel the same way, like I should be laughing hysterically, but my heart feels like ice. A baby? My Roni, who hasn't let me sleep in her bed for more than 4 nights in a row, wants a baby?

I'm completely blindsided, is this really my Roni? Ripples of panic run down my spine.

Shit, is Bruce right? Am I going to lose her if I don't do the marriage and kids thing? Do I want to get married and have kids? Damn it, I don't want to give up this perfect life that I have with Roni. My house. Her house. Our life together and separate.

But I don't want to lose her either.

Fuck, I need to think.

I slowly back away from the sunroom, not hearing anything else that Roni and Val are saying. My mind is too tumultuous to pay attention. I go into the kitchen, make myself a cup of coffee, and send a group text to my friends. Hopefully, a couple of them can take a trip with me. Take the bikes out and maybe head to Ryan's fishing cabin in Louisiana for a long weekend. I get the kettle going, figuring Roni has probably lost her cup of tea or let it get cold, and then make her tea just how she likes it. Steeped for 4 minutes with just a dash of honey.

The guys' replies roll in. Kenny, Ryan, and Nate are good to leave today. The rest will join us early tomorrow morning. I grab the cup of tea and follow the sound of giggles to the love of my life.

"Here you go, Sunflower. I figured your current one was cold by now," I say, kissing her forehead. She smiles at me, accepts the cup, and pats my hand in appreciation.

"Me, Kenny, and the guys are all heading to the fishing cabin this morning. So I'll probably see you Sunday night or Monday evening, depending on when I get back."

"Oh! That sounds like fun! Did I know you had this planned?"

"Nope," I say, "It was a spur-of-the-moment type deal."

"Cool, cool." She says over her steaming cup of tea. "You have a good weekend and be careful. Be sure to come kiss me before you head out."

"Of course, my Sunflower."

Roni

After Quinn kisses me and leaves for his trip, I turn to Val. "Something's up."

They look up from their sketchpad and ask, "How so?"

"I'm not entirely sure. His vibes were off, like he was saying all the right things but acting all wrong. And going on a trip last minute? That's unusual. He also didn't smile or laugh. He's usually one obnoxiously jolly fellow. So that's strange." Anxiety squeezes my heart, making it hard to take a full breath.

"Now that you say something, yeah, I see it. Something was off with him. You think he's mad about us trashing his place last night?"

"Shit. I would be. Jesus Christ on a cranberry cracker. I'm always on some shit about not touching my things, and then I just invite myself in and fuck his shit up? He's going to dump me and move out of that house, and what will I do without Quinn?" I ask, my panic rising.

He's going to leave me.

I'm nothing but a burden to him.

Someone he has to take care of.

He could do so much better than me.

Val claps in front of my face. "No!' they shout at me.

"We aren't going to spiral. We are going to keep busy, letting Quinn process whatever he needs to process, and we'll go from there. But, Roni, look at me. That man is in love with you. He barely looks away from you. I doubt one fuck up is going to change that. I'd bet he was super surprised to find out he was pissed at you and needed to process that. Probably scared the hell out of him, doubt he even thought he could be mad at you."

None of that soothes the panic still building in my chest. My clothes feel too tight, the air conditioner is too loud, and the sun is too bright. I can't do this.

Knowing the tears will fall in about a minute, I stand up and tell Val they should go. Then I walk into my bathroom, turn off the lights, sit on the closed toilet lid, and sob.

He can't possibly love me; I'm terrible. I yelled at him about sunflowers when all he was trying to do was cut my grass. Like I asked him to. What did he see in me, anyway? A strange woman living in the woods. I bet he's out there cheating on me. I'd deserve it. Why should he be loyal when I am such a burden? He can't touch my shit but I destroy his?

And on and on and on. Sometimes, like now, it's impossible to stop the negative thoughts. I must find a quiet, dark, small space and let it happen. I grab my notebook and pour out all of my toxic thoughts.

After an hour or so, I finally snap out of it. I shakily stand up and turn on my shower. I glance in the mirror, taking in my puffy eyes and flushed skin. I'm a goddamn mess. Before the negativity can take over, again, I go find my Bluetooth speaker, turn on some fun poppy dance music, and sing my way into the shower. I let the scalding water run over me until it turns cold, and then I get out.

I'm still anxious, but there is nothing that can be done at the moment.

I walk down the hall into my living room and find Val reading on the sofa.

"I thought I asked you to go home?"

"You did, I didn't listen."

"Obviously."

I glare at them, and they smile as they dog-ear a battered historical romance novel and put it back on my shelf.

"So, now that we have established you kicking me out and me not going, what are we doing this weekend?"

I collapse on the sofa next to them and say, "Will you tell me that everything is going to be ok and Quinn isn't going to dump me? Move out and leave me here by myself?"

They chuckle and say, "Of course, everything is going to be ok. It's Quinn; he is absolutely enchanted by you. What is that line from Pride and Prejudice? You have bewitched his heart and all that jazz or whatever Mr. Darcy said. I think he is just upset that we trashed his house and doesn't know how to deal with feeling that emotion towards you."

"I just wish he would talk to me."

"I'm sure he will. I think he just needed to get his thoughts in order. The man has proved that he would rather saw off his own arm than hurt you. I wonder if he was worried he might snap at you or something, so he's cooling off, and then y'all will talk, and everything will be fine."

"Thank you," I said, sniffling, my eyes watering again.

"Oh, hell no! Get up, get dressed. We are going...somewhere!"

"Where?"

"I don't know! We'll decide after you are dressed!"

Quinn

I thought the ride or some fishing would calm my mind and let me think. I was wrong. I just kept replaying the wedding Pinterest board and her saying she wants a baby the whole ride. I just feel more confused, hurt, and scared than before. Roni is my life now, but we had an agreement, goddamn it. What will I do if she changes the rules? Can I let her go to preserve my life? Can I even be happily married with babies? I'm not much more than a decade from retiring. I was looking forward to more time with Roni. Not Little League and ballet. But her devastation when she thought I was cheating on her, and how insecure in the relationship she felt. Who am I to deny her this added security if she needs it?

"Alright, fucker. Spill. What's wrong with you?" Kenny asks, slinging his legs over the edge of the pier. We just sit there for a moment, looking at the murky water.

"I think Roni wants a baby."

Kenny bursts into laughter.

I elbow him in the side. "It's not funny, asshole."

Kenny, barely controlling himself, asks, "What are you talking about? Roni does not want kids. When Rhonda got pregnant the first time, Roni offered condolences before realizing we were happy. She looked shocked that we were intentionally having a baby. Rhonda said she just about fell out when she told her about this one. No way that woman wants a baby."

"I thought so, too. But I heard her and Val talking. She specifically said she wanted a baby. And she's planning a wedding using that photo app. I didn't stick around for that talk. I came out here instead. I gotta figure out what I'm going to do, and fast."

"Look, are you sure what you heard? That just doesn't sound like Roni." Kenny says, scratching the back of his neck and squinting at the sun. He reaches into his shirt pocket, pulls out a pack of cigarettes, and offers me one. I quit ages ago, but shit, this feels like a good time to pick up the habit again. I light the cigarette and take that first puff, the smoke burning down my throat. A whisper of calm circles my brain as I exhale.

"Yeah, man, no way to misunderstand what I heard. She literally said, 'I want a cute, chunky baby with fat rolls.' Like nothing to get wrong."

Bruce laughs behind me, fuck that guy, and slaps my back as he sits on the other side of me.

"I told you, dude. I fucking told you. These bitches always want marriage and babies. Get them all loved up, and you are trapped." Bruce says, still chuckling. "You are so screwed."

I roar, "Don't call Roni a bitch!" and shove him into the brown water below. Kenny slaps me on the back of my head and tells me, "You know that isn't what he meant, asshole," as Bruce pops out of the water, sputtering and pissed off.

"What the fuck, douchebag? This water is cold!"

I don't answer and I definitely don't apologize. The son of a bitch had it coming for a long time. As Bruce pulls himself out of the water with Kenny lending a hand, he wipes his face and says, "Don't worry, I won't hold a grudge if you invite me to the wedding."

Then the asshole just walks away laughing, leaving a trail of water behind him.

"Fuck!" I yell at the Spanish moss-covered trees. Then I take a deep breath, turn to Kenny, and say, "Well, I guess I'm getting married. I'm not going to lose her. Help me pick out a ring?"

"Whoa, why don't you sit on it for a minute? Think about it a bit; maybe just talk to Roni."

"Sometimes it takes Roni a while to figure out what she feels. I mean, I knew she loved me like two months before she did. But it stresses her out before she figures it out. What if I can just lift that stress? Go ahead and propose. Get that out of the way, and we can figure out the rest afterward. Besides that, I know she will agonize over how to tell me when she made such a big deal out of never living together."

"Yeah, I can see that. I just, she's always been so skittish, and I worry about you scaring her off or something."

"Trust me, I don't want to scare her off either, but I don't think I will. I think I will take a stressor off her plate."

"Well, alrighty then. I think there is a mall up the road a bit. I'm sure we can find something at that jewelry store." Kenny says with a sigh.

We sit silently, watching the sunset over the river with the Spanish moss swaying in the breeze. I can feel Kenny's concern, but it doesn't change my mind. The more I turn this over in my mind, the more certain I become. Roni is planning a wedding on that app and Roni said, out loud, that she wants a baby. My Sunflower has never even joked about getting married or having kids, why would she start fantasizing now? Unless her mind has changed. We are doing so well, get along so great, maybe that changed her mind?

My heart warms at the mere idea that I love her so well that she changes her mind about marriage and babies. Then, it freezes when I consider what that all actually means. How will we combine our homes?

I don't want to give up my freedom for children.

"If Rhonda didn't want to get married and have kids, would you have given all that up just to be with her?" I ask Kenny, startling him out of his thoughts.

"I don't know. I mean, I obviously would give up anything for that woman. And now that we have Sarah and the baby on the way, I wouldn't give them up for anything, so that's hard to answer. But part of the reason Rhonda and I fell in love is we both wanted the same things. That bonded us. If suddenly Rhonda changed her views on things, wouldn't that make her not the woman I fell in love with? Fuck man, that is a hard question to answer."

"I know. Man, Roni is my everything, but the Roni I fell in love with wouldn't want to live with me. Wouldn't want to get married. Wouldn't want to have kids." I want to cry. My world feels like it's caving in.

"All I can say is imagine your life with Roni and kids and all that, and then imagine your life if you break it off with Roni now. Which one would you prefer?"

I don't even think before I say, "Roni. I would prefer any kind of life with Roni."

"Well, there you have it. Looks like you are getting hitched," Kenny says, still worried, "But maybe you should talk to Roni first. Let her know you are okay with getting married. Don't just spring this on her."

"The conversation will stress her out, and I just want to make her life better. I don't want her to stress over anything to do with me. If I propose, it will prove to her that I am completely willing to marry her. Instead of her agonizing over whether I was just saying that or if I meant it. If it is my idea, she will never have a moment of doubt. Ultimately, I don't want her to stress, and I never want her to think I didn't want to marry her."

"But you don't," Kenny says.

"Why should she know that? Would you want Rhonda to know if you didn't want to marry her but did it to make her happy? Especially if you knew you would be happy to have Rhonda however you could?"

Kenny sighs, "Alright, man. You convinced me. I don't feel good about this but you know I'll help y'all however I can."

Chapter 28
A crossed witch.

Roni

I'm plundering around the store buying crap I don't need when I get a call from Quinn. My heart is pounding as I answer it, "Hey, you."

"Hey, yourself. I'm home. Are you going to be here soon?"

Oh my God.

Breathe.

"Uh, yeah. I'll be there in about 45 minutes. I'll see you then?"

"Of course."

He didn't sound mad. But maybe he was just resolved? Decided.

Only one way to find out.

As the cashier rings up my junk, my heart feels wrapped in a too-tight cage. My smile and polite thanks feel brittle. The sun is too bright, and I can't breathe through the humidity. I toss my bags into the passenger seat as I sit in my sweltering Jeep. I crank up the AC and try to calm my breathing.

Thoughts of running away race through my mind. Leave him before he can leave me.

But I know I can't do that. Since my parents' deaths, I haven't let anyone get close enough to abandon me until Quinn. The thought of living without him makes me nauseous. His smiling face is as precious and necessary to me as Ginger, Val, and my family. He is one of my few constants.

I tell myself that Quinn won't leave me as I throw my truck in gear and leave the parking lot.

Quinn won't leave me.

Quinn won't leave me.

Quinn won't leave me.

I chant repeatedly until I pull onto my red dirt driveway.

Quinn

Roni's Jeep pulls into the driveway, so I get in my place across from the front door so she can see me when she walks in. I hear her step in front of the door and imagine her slender hand reaching for the door handle.

I feel like I am going to vomit as I go down on one knee. One unwanted marriage seems like enough for a lifetime, but I want her. However I can have her. Hell, if Amanda had not trapped me with a fake ultrasound, I'd probably be begging to marry Roni. If marriage and babies were the tolls for sleeping beside her, for getting to be near her every day, then I would pay it.

Her beautiful face appears as the door opens.

"Veronica Corbin, I love you more than I have ever thought possible. I want to be with you for the rest of our lives. Will you marry me?'

She gasps and howls like a crossed witch, "What have you done?" Her hand swings back before she knocks the ring from my hand and across the room.

My mind refuses to process the scene before my eyes as I remain frozen, one knee still on the rug. She quickly reaches down and scoops up Ginger before running out the door. Running? Fuck! I stand up and race out the open front door to see a cloud of dust and the taillights of her orange jeep racing down the road.

I survey the small cottage. What just happened? The cat is gone. My legs give out and I drop to my knees as the reality of the situation hits me.

She took the cat.

Fuck.

What have I done?

Roni

I can't breathe.

I can't breathe.

I can't breathe.

I have to get away. I can't stay here. This town, this area, this whole state has me in its claustrophobic grip. I drive until I hit the next town and pull into the Walmart parking lot.

Breathe, Roni.

In and out.

In and out.

Damn it. I'm going to throw up. I'm losing him.

I put the car in drive and follow the road behind Walmart, heading towards the high school. Brian should be home and won't mind Ginger hanging out until... until I figure something out.

I start to sob as I think of leaving Quinn.

But he was supposed to know me, really know me. He promised.

I don't recall the drive to my brother's house, but suddenly, I am pulling in his driveway.

I knock on my brother's door, the cat in my arms and tears streaming down my face. He opens the door with a smile that quickly shutters to concern.

"V-baby, what's wrong? Are you ok? Is Quinn ok?" Sobs bubble up so hard that I feel dizzy from lack of air. My chest feels like it's caving in. Brian tugs me inside and takes Ginger out of my arms. Within minutes, I find myself on his sofa, a hot cup of tea on the table beside me, and Brian sitting across from me, looking worried.

"V-baby, I've never seen you like this. Lisa is on her way, thought maybe having another girl around would be nice, but I think she's called the whole gang. Sorry!" He flinches, waiting for me to panic, but instead, I soggily laugh.

"Well, I've never needed the girl gang to sort through love bullshit, so I guess I owe them."

Anger flashes across Brian's face as he asks, "Did Quinn hurt you? I'm going to kill him."

The knife in my chest twists as I say, "No, he didn't hurt me. He proposed. Fucking proposed. We were perfect, goddamn it! I thought neither of us wanted marriage and all that. How could he do this to me?"

"Oh, honey," Brian says as he wraps his arms around me. "Would marriage be so bad? It's obvious how much you love him."

"It would be to me. I don't want to live with him. I need my space; I need my time alone. I thought he hated the whole idea of marriage. That's why we worked so well. That's why I love him so much. We were right next door to each other. It was perfect." I wail as Brian awkwardly pats my shoulder, not used to emotional outbursts from me. Soon enough, the front door opens, and the women in my family pour in, some with snacks and others with booze.

Quinn

Fuck.

My knees ache as I stand up on the front porch of the love of my life's house. I feel numb and panicked, and I can't breathe. I hobble in the house, frantically searching for my phone. I have to call her. I have to speak to her before she leaves town. Phone in hand, I press call only to hear her ringtone from the basket by the front door.

Thank God. Her wallet and phone are here. She can't leave town without those.

Think. Where would she go with nothing but a cat and in a panic?

Brian.

Of course.

She was the closest to him and his wife, even though she was close to all of them. She said that she would run to Brian whenever she spiraled as a child. I grab her a change of clothes, Ginger's food and litter, and purse and run out to my bike. I almost don't want to bring her things. I don't want to make it easy for her to skip town, but I can't stand her not having what she needs.

It's a miracle that I don't get a speeding ticket on my way to her brother's house. I round the last corner and park across the street.

Her jeep is there.

Thank fuck.

I lean against my bike and call Brian.

"Quinn, what did you do, bro?"

"I lost my goddamn mind for a minute. Is she ok? Is she staying with you? Please don't let her leave town. Please. I need a chance to talk to her. Would she talk to me? Now? I just..."

"Hey, hey, calm down. She's not running. All the women are on their way here and bringing booze. They'll talk her off the ledge tonight, get her trashed, and then you come by tomorrow afternoon and talk to her. I'm sure she'll be mostly over the hangover by then," he chuckles like my life isn't falling apart.

"Ok, I'll do that. Can you come out here and grab her stuff? I brought Ginger's stuff and Roni's purse and shit."

"Just sit it on the porch. I don't want them to know you're out there."

"Will do."

Chapter 29
Booze is here, bitches.

Roni

"Booze is here, bitches!" Lisa says as she flings the front door open. Her and Brian's 21-year-old daughter, Brit, follows behind her, carrying a box full of bottles from the ABC Store.

"Thank goodness it's not a Sunday." Brit chuckles behind her mom.

"I sent out a Bitchin' and Witchin' group text, so we'll be invaded pretty soon. I don't think anyone had to work today." Lisa says as she unloads the bottles onto the kitchen counter.

"I guess that's my cue to leave," Brian says as he kisses his wife and daughter, then makes his way over to me for one of his perfect bear hugs. Damn, I love my brother. His hugs are almost as good as Quinn's hugs.

No.

I'm not going to think like that. But my eyes are already filling with tears. Fuck. Just the thought of him breaks my heart all over again.

"Oh, baby." Lisa whispers as she pushes a Crown n' Coke into my hands.

I take a couple of big sips and let the burn pull me back into this moment with my sister-in-law.

Just then, the front door opens again, showing my sisters, Bex and Janie, with two of my sisters-in-law, Carmen and Joan. Carmen is looking at her phone and says, "Robin, Bethany, and Mac will be here in about 10 minutes. They stopped by Wal-Mart for mixers and shit."

I have to laugh at that. Looks like the men are on their own tonight. The ladies are getting fucked up. Especially since Robin, who has been married to my brother for 26 years, is coming. That woman drinks like a fish, has no filter, and raised a rowdy daughter just like her. My niece Mac is 21 and can probably hold her liquor better than all of us. Luckily, my brother's daughter from his first marriage, Bethany, is also coming. She's just about the only one who can handle Robin and Mac when the booze comes out. Even Anthony can't get them to behave.

Janie sits down next to me. As the oldest, she has always been a motherly figure to me. Hell, our parents died when I was 14, and she finished raising me. She wraps me in her arms, and I just break down. Sobbing on her shoulder as if the world is ending, and to me, it very well might be. "Oh, V-baby, whatever it is, we'll figure it out. Or we'll help you hide the body. Whatever you need." Before I can reply, the front door bursts open again, and in stomps Robin,

Mac, and Bethany. Well, Robin and Mac stomp in. Bethany walks like a lady and gently shuts the door, a worried look coming over her face as she looks at me. Bethany and I have always been close, with me just four years older than her. I thought she was my own personal baby doll when Ant's first wife brought her home from the hospital.

"Okay, why are you crying? Shit, I haven't seen you cry since you were 14, and we moved you in with Janie," Robin asks as she sits on the other side of me, a full bottle of tequila in her hand. I unwrap from Janie and take a deep breath.

"Quinn proposed."

The roar of "What the hell?" and "I thought y'all weren't into marriage?" and "What has gotten into him?" was deafening. Everyone is talking at once and I have not had enough liquor to be cool with this noise.

Luckily, Mac is of the same mindset. "Yall, shut the fuck up!" she yells and a hush falls over the room. I mouth 'Thank you.' and she sends me a wink.

"Well, what did he say after you told him no?" Bethany asks.

"I don't know," I say, looking at the floor and folding my arms around my waist.

"How do you not know? Did he get pissed and leave?"

"I left," I mumble without raising my eyes.

"Holy shit, you dumb broad." Robin laughs. "You didn't even find out why he was asking or his plan before you worked yourself into this state?"

"I panicked! I grabbed the cat and my keys and ran! Oh, Jesus Christ, on a cranberry cracker, I slapped the ring out of his hand, grabbed the cat, and ran." I whisper while covering my face with my hands. Damn, I am stupid. When I look up, they're all trying not to laugh. Bex's face is tomato red, and I can hear Mac and Robin laughing in the kitchen.

As soon as I make eye contact, Bex starts cackling, which gets everyone else started.

"She just grabbed the cat and ran!" I hear Robin snort from behind me. Even Janie and sweet Bethany are gasping for air after that one.

"Okay, so let's get this straight. Quinn went down on one knee and proposed. You then knocked the ring out of his hand, grabbed Ginger, and ran away?"

I sigh, "Yeah, pretty much. It was a really sweet proposal, too. I love him. I don't want to lose him. But I can't have a stinky boy living in my house. He's always touching stuff and trying to clean up my tea cups. Drives me crazy. We'd be divorced within the year."

This starts the laughter again, with jokes about my habit of abandoning tea cups and how messy my room is despite no stinky boys living with me.

Once everyone has calmed down, Janie asks, "Okay, what are we going to do about this? Are we getting totally shit-faced tonight and dealing with the fallout tomorrow? Dealing with it all tonight? Or are we sipping, getting tipsy and giggly while we discuss this mess and then dealing with it tomorrow?"

"Tipsy and giggly," I decid quickly. "I don't want to be dealing with a hangover and trying to convince my boyfriend that our lives are great and we don't need to do...that," I say, gagging while my sisters laugh at me.

Quinn

I'm two shots deep at the bar when Kenny and Brian walk in - both wearing matching expressions of pity. My heart fractures as I wonder if Roni said something to put that expression on her brother's face.

"Has she said something? What do you know?" I demand.

Brian holds his hands up. "Calm down, man. I don't know anything. The chicks kicked me out of the house once the lushes started pouring in," he says with a chuckle.

"Sorry, fuck." I say as I take another shot, my plan to be absolutely obliterated just beginning.

Four hours later, we are shit-faced and planning on heading out when Bruce comes strolling in. I'm irrationally pissed at this motherfucker for putting ridiculous ideas in my head. "You asshole. I proposed, and she left!"

Bruce barks out a laugh and says, "Oh, shit? Really? Maybe I should go find her, see if she needs some... consoling."

I see red as my fist flies straight into his nose. The crunching sound and blood spurting soothe my wounded soul. Unfortunately, my rage just isn't enough to keep me going and the sight of Bruce's fist is the last thing I remember before everything goes black.

Chapter 30

Titties bouncing around the pokey.

Roni

I'm mostly sober and snuggled up on my brother's couch with Val, who showed up right after we started drinking with a joint and a promise to help me bury Quinn's body if it came down to it. The high wore off a couple of hours ago and we watched one of my favorite movies. My sisters and nieces are sprawled out all over the place in various stages of sobriety.

I'm dozing off when I hear a phone ringing. All of us sit straight up. It's 2 AM. No one should be calling this late. Lisa answers and almost immediately starts laughing while assuring the caller that she'll be there in a minute. She hangs up the phone, still laughing, and looks at me. "Want to ride down to the jail and bail out your brother and boyfriend?"

"What the fuck?"

She's still laughing when she says "That was Sarah at the police station. She recognized Brian and Quinn and figured she'd call me.

Our boys and Kenny apparently beat the shit out of Bruce down at Travis's and they're completely trashed. She said if we can get up there to bail them out in the next hour or so we won't have to wait around or anything."

"Well, hell. Let me get my shoes on." I say as I kick pillows, blankets and sisters out of the way.

"You might want to put on a bra, too," Janie calls from the kitchen, where she is making a couple of travel mugs of coffee for us to drink en route.

"Yeah, yeah. Everyone loves titties until they start bouncing around at the pokey." I joke while trying to find my bra.

"Pokey? What's a pokey?" Mac asks with a look of disgust on her face.

Robin cackles and replies, "It's what old ladies call the jailhouse."

"Fuck off." I laugh as I throw a pillow at Robin's face, only to realize my bra is somehow attached to it.

"Toss me my bra, would you?" I ask as Robin bats the pillow away.

"Ewe," she says, looking at my industrial-sized and shaped bra. "Why would Quinn want to lock you down so bad if you wear granny bras? Jesus Christ, there are four clasps on the back of this thing."

"Shut up. The gals are massive and must be hoisted up using hard-core machinery. And Quinn doesn't have a problem with them or their machinery."

"Okay, children. We have to go bust the boys out of the pokey, so put your bra on and get in the car." Lisa says with a chuckle as she grabs her keys.

I snap my bra into place, situate the gals, and slide my shoes on.

"Bring me a souvenir!" Val says drowsily from the sofa.

"Such as?" I ask, wondering what they could want from there.

"Mm, surprise me!"

"Sure thing, babe," I say as I shut the front door behind me.

I call Rhonda on the way to the jail to let her know what's up and that we'll snag Kenny for her, but she insists on meeting us up there. Says she really just wants to see Kenny locked up since he's always been such a good boy, never rowdy or anything.

Her calling her grown-ass husband a good boy has Lisa and me cackling for the rest of the drive to the police station.

We wait in the car until Rhonda pulls in next to us about 10 minutes later and then all three of us head inside. Sarah grins at us as she gathers the paperwork.

Quinn

Fuck, my face hurts. At least my nose isn't broken. I can't believe that asshole knocked me out. You know what, no; he didn't knock me out. I was wasted and fixing to pass out anyway. From being drunk. Not from that pussy ass punch. I glance at Kenny and Brian. They barely look like they were in a fight. Bruce, on the other hand, is looking a little... well, fuck. He looks like he got his ass beaten. I wouldn't know. Since I passed out. From being drunk. Of course.

My body goes numb as I remember why I was so drunk.

Roni.

I wonder if I can keep from seeing her until my face isn't so messed up.

But if I do that I could lose her.

Fuck.

Okay, if I ice it down once I get home and wait until the evening to see her, maybe it won't be so bad.

I hear giggling down the hall that sounds suspiciously like...

I whip my head to the side, looking straight into Brian's face. He looks amused, and a little confused.

"Who did you call to bail us out?" I ask as the door opens. The most beautiful woman in the world is staring in shock and giggling at my face.

Everyone else fades away as I stand up. It feels like years since I've looked into her laughing eyes. I start towards her as she flings herself into my arms.

Home. This woman in my arms, her magical giggles against my neck.

This is home.

Roni

I wake up slowly, the stress, booze, and pot of the day before making me sluggish. Judging by the light filtering in through the curtains, it must be late afternoon. My heart warms as I feel Quinn squeeze me tighter to his chest, his breath still even, wanting me close even in sleep. I kiss his shoulder, the closest part of his body to my mouth, and try to extract myself from his arms. We have got to talk soon, and I need coffee to get going. And I'm going to have to hunt down a sports drink and Tylenol for Mr. Fistfight.

Then we have to talk. My heart hurts just thinking about the upcoming conversation.

"No, Sunflower, stay," he mumbles in his rough morning voice.

"I'm just getting my coffee going. Then I'll come back."

"No, please. Just let me hold you a little longer. I was so scared yesterday. I thought I'd lost you. I thought you'd just leave town, not looking back." He says into my neck, punctuating each sentence with a kiss.

"Quinn, I would never leave you without looking back. You are the great love of my life."

"And you are mine, Sunflower. Fine. Go get coffee," he says, slapping my ass as he rolls us over so we can get out of bed.

A few minutes later, our coffee is ready and Quinn and I are sitting at the table, putting off the conversation that we need to have. He's chugged a couple of electrolyte drinks and taken some Tylenol; I've checked his bandage and applied more antiseptic cream. We've brushed our teeth and stared longingly at each other.

Time to rip the bandaid off.

"Okay, Quinn. What the actual fuck?"

"Shit, babe. I thought I was going to lose you."

I stare at him incredulously. Has he not heard a damn word I've ever said? I start to feel my poor heart break even more as my eyes fill with tears. He finally looks up from his coffee and, in an instant, has me pulled into his lap.

"My Sunflower. I'm so sorry. I know. I know you! But I let that fucker Bruce into my head. He kept going on and on about how women always want to get married and how his girl didn't want to get married until she left him because he wouldn't propose and I just can't lose you. But I kept telling him, I knew you didn't want marriage. You would tell me if you did. But then I saw your wedding planning app and then I heard you and Val talking about wanting a baby, I thought you were hinting! I don't want to get married, but I don't want to lose you! I would have done anything."

"When were we talking about wanting a baby? I've never talked about wanting a baby."

"The day after you and Val got trashed. Y'all were up early talking about wanting a fat baby."

I burst out laughing, "Holy fuck. Dude, you know Rhonda is pregnant, and I want her to have a fat baby, so I can cuddle and nap with that baby. I do not want one of my own. I'm vaguely disturbed that her and Kenny chose to have two kids but I dig a squishy baby."

Quinn looks both relieved and terrified, so I decide to put him out of his misery. The poor idiot.

"Okay. Okay. So, you don't want to marry me? You don't want to have babies with me? And you don't want to live with me? Do I have that right?"

"God, no! I love our lives just as they are. This, what we have, is exactly what I want."

"Then stop fucking it up!"

He laughs at that and kisses me, and all is perfect again.

Quinn calls in some vacation time and we spend the next week wrapped up in each other. Usually in bed. But sometimes in my papasan, a few times on the kitchen table, and once among my sunflowers.

I'm in the kitchen cooking dinner when Quinn walks in, smacks my ass, kisses my temple, and sits at the table.

"Sunflower, can we talk for a minute?"

"Of course," I say, wiping my hands on my apron and sitting across from him.

"Well, since we aren't going to get married, I would still like for us to have the benefits. Especially in medical situations. I want you to make any and all medical choices that I can't. You'll inherit my life insurance and everything else. Just like if we were married. You are it for me."

"Quinn Bernard Evans, you are it for me too," I say, grinning over at him. He scowls and shakes his head.

"Please take this seriously, dearest."

"I am. Your middle name is serious business. Besides that, yes. Let's do it. Maybe we can make an appointment tomorrow and set all of this up on both sides. I'm excited to have all the benefits without that marriage nonsense."

"You just don't want to live with me," Quinn says, leaning over to kiss me.

"That, too." I chuckle, "Speaking of, I will need you to go home after dinner. I need at least three days to recover from our fuck-fest."

He laughs and says, "I knew that was coming, I'm surprised you lasted a week."

"It just flew by. I enjoy having you in my house, surprisingly. Almost enough to reconsider moving in. But I really need to be alone to recharge and prefer having a whole house to be alone in."

"I know, baby. I feel the same way, except I just need to get out of your cluttered house."

"It's not cluttered! It's maximalist."

"Whatever you say, Sunflower. Anyways, I figured you'd kick me out today, so I made plans with the guys to play poker at Kenny's tonight. I'll be heading that way after dinner."

"Perfect!" I say as I dish up our dinner, cornbread, and lima beans, and sit a plate in front of him.

We eat in comfortable silence, as we've always eaten together, and a wave of relief washes over me that everything turned out okay. That Quinn loves me so much that he would give up his freedom, his home, just to make me happy. The ring he bought crosses my mind.

Did he return it?

I kind of want it. Not as an engagement ring, god no, but as a reminder of his devotion. I want to wear it around my neck.

Can I ask him for it? Is the ring tainted? I don't think so. Will he hate seeing it around my neck? A shiver of unease rushes over my skin, tears sting my eyes. I look at my plate, blinking rapidly, hoping Quinn is too enthralled in his dinner to notice.

"Hey, Sunflower, what's wrong?" Quinn asks, reaching across the table to grab my hand.

"I want the ring," I mumble, feeling his hand tense in mine, dread washing over me in waves.

Quinn barks out a laugh, "That damn engagement ring? The one that almost sent you running for the hills?"

I look up at him, seeing nothing but amusement and love in his eyes. "Yes, that one. I want to wear it on a necklace. I might not want to get married or live together, but that ring really symbolizes your devotion to me. What you will sacrifice for me. I want it by my heart, always."

His precious eyes turn glassy before he rapidly blinks and coughs before saying, "Well, shit, Sunflower. I never even looked for the ring after you knocked it out of my hand. Let me go see if I can find it in your mess of a living room."

"Oh, fuck," I laugh, getting up to help him hunt.

We spend twenty minutes on our hands and knees looking under bookcases and papasan chairs, only to find it between the cushions of my sofa. I hurry to my room to get my mother's chain and return, clasping the jewelry around my neck. I straddle Quinn's lap and ask, "What do you think?"

"Beautiful, just like you," he says, kissing me slowly and thoroughly before slapping my ass and saying, "Hop up hot stuff. I have to go over to my place before heading to Kenny's. I'll swing back by before I head out, gotta get one last kiss, you know."

"Make sure you do."

He leans over, kisses me, and goes out the door.

Chapter 31
Put your dick away.

Quinn

I let myself into Roni's house, intent on getting one last kiss before my night out with the boys. Okay, so it's less of a night out and more of a hanging out at Kenny's house while his kids are at Rhonda's mom's house.

"Alright, Sunflower. I'm heading out, I'll see you tomorrow." I say as I lean down to give Roni a kiss goodbye. She's a little distracted, wrapped up in a romance novel, munching on sour gummy worms, but she looks up and gives me a kiss.

"I love you," she says, and warmth runs through my body as sunbursts interrupt my vision. Just like it does every time she says those magical words to me.

"I love you, too"

"See you tomorrow, Quinn Eugene Evans!" she says, laughing.

I freeze.

She laughs harder, "Oh my god. Seriously? Eugene? And you got your panties in a twist over Carl? Holy cow."

I growl and kiss her smiling lips, taking my time to savor every second.

"I was named after my uncle. It's a fine name."

"Yes, yes. A lovely name. So glad that we aren't having children, your idea of a fine name kind of sucks."

"Oh, hush, woman. I've gotta go. Can't bicker with you all day."

"Okay, Eugene, bye!"

I throw my middle finger in the air as I walk out of her door, listening to her snort-laughing after me.

Roni

A text from Quinn interrupts my reading.

> i see yo bros duck

> Brian has a duck?

> duck

duck

d ik

caulk

rooster

duck

fuck

Are you trying to say that you saw Brian's dick/cock?

Yes! An kenny U win

You are looking at Kenny and Brian's dicks and I win?

big u win big

How so?

I big, u win

Holy cow. Did y'all measure dicks?

ye im biggst

Congratulations. Never tell me about Kenny and Brian's dicks again.

do not think abut other caulks

caulks

I wouldn't think about other cocks if you didn't mention them.

damn it

Put your dick away. I love you.

love you more

I sit my phone down, chuckling. Boys are so gross. Why would they even think to measure dick size? Not once in all my years of having friends have we ever measured our clits. Hell, I don't know what any of my chick friend's hoo-has look like. Shrugging off my thoughts of gross boys and chick clits, I meander into my kitchen to figure out my dinner and a cup of tea. Fixing myself a little fruit and cheese plate and a nice iced peach tea, I start the hunt for my book. I know the last time I read it was this afternoon when Quinn left, but it's not in the sunroom.

Where did I sit the damn thing?

Unable to find my book, I switch to plan B. Movie night. I'm feeling some snarky Woody Harrelson, so Zombieland it is. I set up my iPad on my TV tray table, move my annoyed feline, gather my goodies, and settle into my papasan chair for a nice little sloth night. The movie is almost finished when my phone alerts me to multiple text messages pouring in. Seeing they're from Rhonda, I open it and laugh.

I caught Quinn being cute, so I snagged some pictures and a video for you.

The video is first, in it is Quinn, slurring his words, showing Brian, Kenny, and a few other men selfies of us and explaining exactly what we were doing when we took them. I feel like the Grinch, with my heart swelling at least 3 sizes, just watching his sweet face as he talks about us. About me. Tears prick as the video ends, and I look at the photos. Quinn is lying on the floor, with his phone propped against a pillow beside him. I wonder what he's watching that made Rhonda snap this photo, then the next picture comes in and I don't have to wonder anymore. It's a photo of me, asleep in bed, that I had no idea he had taken. Rhonda sends one final text that says, 'He was complaining about not getting to kiss you goodnight and that he'd rather be sleeping next to you. Then he propped his phone up and said 'That's better.' It was so sweet.'

My heart aches when I miss him. What a strange sensation. I rarely miss people. Most of the time, I forget that they even exist. But not Quinn. I consider picking him up but decide against it.

I miss him, but I need time alone. I need to sleep alone now and then. It's been about a week since we've slept apart. We needed that time together after the devastation his proposal caused, but now it's time to get back to our regular lives.

Quinn

I check again, to make sure I have everything on this random ass list Roni gave me. Crackers, Ginger Ale, strawberry ice cream, lemon juice, Wickle Pickles, ketchup, 3 mangos, and a carton of blueberries. Next time I get too drunk to go home, I will not call Roni to see if she needs anything from the store the next day. Took me about 3 years to find lemon juice. I thought it was a cooking thing, not a drinking juice thing. I grab a couple of bags of my favorite chips, some dip, and a few other snacky things and then head to check out. Damn, these lines are long. I pick the shortest one and end up behind Philip, Roni's nephew.

"Hey, man, how's it going?" I ask when he glances my way.

"Oh, hey! Everything is good on my end. How're you guys? I haven't seen Roni in a while," he says, perusing my cart.

"We're great. We should have another bonfire, get the families together soon."

"That sounds great," he says, distractedly, still looking in my cart. "Listen, is Roni pregnant?" He whispers, gesturing to my cart.

I crack up, "Absolutely not! Hell, if Roni were pregnant, she'd be on the phone with Planned Parenthood while giving me a vasectomy with a rusty pair of scissors and you know it!"

Philip starts laughing while the elderly lady behind me shushes us and says that we were being inappropriate. Which only makes us laugh more.

Oops.

I finally manage to get home and start unloading Roni's bullshit when I hear her come out onto the porch and glare at me.

"Whoa, what have I done?"

"Really, Quinn? A vasectomy with rusty scissors? You said that to my nephew?"

I start laughing again as I set her groceries on her kitchen table. "Well, yeah. Did I lie?"

She smirks, "Probably not."

I pull her against me, her soft lips meet mine, I slide my hand down to her ass to grab and jiggle it, "Where's my dinner, woman?" I growl against her lips.

Her snort-laugh rings out, sending tingles over my skin, as I smile against her lips.

"It's on the stove. Go fix yourself a plate."

"God, woman, I love you so much."

Another snort-laugh, "Not as much as you love my cooking, apparently."

That stops me in my tracks and I spin around. "You could never cook again and I would still love you. I would probably be really sad and hungry, but you are the one thing I can't live without."

"Okay, don't make me cry over burgers." She fans her face with her hand delicately.

"Nothing but the truth, Sunflower."

Roni

Our dinner is a boisterous affair, with Quinn sharing all the drunk shenanigans from last night and me laughing until I have tears running down my face. Once we finish eating and handle the dishes, I kiss Quinn and go out back to tend my garden for a bit. The sun is setting; the whole yard is glowing as I dig up my potatoes. A lawn chair creaks as Quinn sits down armed with his guitar. He plays one of my favorite songs after winking and blowing me a kiss. I never thought being serenaded was hot, but this? A large, sexy man playing my favorite songs as the sun sets and I do something I love? If I wasn't already hopelessly in love with this man, I would be now.

A few songs later, when the moon is out, Quinn stops playing and says, "Want to get cleaned up and go into town for milkshakes?"

"Oh! Yes! Sonic?"

"Of course."

I skip over to him, careful not to get any dirt on him, and give him a kiss before going inside. I shower quickly and pull my wild, towel-dried hair into a braid before pulling on jeans and a t-shirt. I walk barefoot into the living room to find Quinn holding Ginger like a newborn and rocking her.

"Shhh, the baby is sleeping," He says, smiling.

I slid my feet into my shoes, giggling, and then take the grumpy gal from Quinn. She makes a threatening sound, so I quickly dump her on the back of the sofa and walk into Quinn's arms.

"Ready to go?"

"Yup."

The drive goes by fast, with both of us singing along to the radio, Quinn's hand on my thigh. We get our milkshakes and sit in the truck, holding hands, kissing, and laughing.

"You said we were getting milkshakes. A Sonic Blast is ice cream."

"At least I didn't get a boring strawberry milkshake like some gorgeous woman I know."

"Flattery will get you nowhere when you talk shit on my milkshake. And it's strawberry cheesecake, not plain strawberry. Thank you very much." I say, sticking my nose up in the air.

"But, baby, I love you. You're so pretty and beautiful and hot and sexy and gorgeous." He says like we're in a bar and he's trying to sweet talk me into bed.

I giggle and watch his eyes light up. "Fine, flattery will get you a spot in my bed tonight, big boy."

"That's all I've ever wanted," He says, wriggling his eyebrows.

"That's it?"

"Well, that and just you and your cooking."

"I love you," I say, leaning over for a kiss.

"I will love you until the day I die, Sunflower."

Chapter 32

Dead grandmother. Get it together.

Quinn

A sudden knock on the door wakes us. The clock on the bedside table shows 3 AM. I quickly rise and reach for the baseball bat I convinced Roni to keep behind the bedroom door.

Seems like I am destined to fight all intruders on Roni's property in nothing but my boxer briefs.

"Who's there?" I snarl, growl, yell at the front door.

"I need Ver-Ver." I hear Val sob from the other side. I quickly toss the bat onto the sofa and fling open the door, with Roni behind me. Val, face red and tears streaming down to the neck, glances over their shoulder and waves at the red truck that reverses out of the driveway and leaves. They walk right into Roni's arms, sobbing, "Memaw's dead."

I leave them crying in the entryway, making a couple of cups of tea and snacks and sitting them on the bedside table in Roni's room. I

gently pull my people into the bedroom and get them situated with
Pride and Prejudice playing on the tablet for background noise. I
kiss Roni on the lips and Val on the forehead before turning to
leave. Val sobs out, "Quinn, where the fuck are you going? I need
you, too."

Fuck, my heart.

"Y'all want me to stay?" I ask with my heart in my throat.

Roni looks at me and says, "Duh. But maybe grab the booze, just
in case."

"Yes, booze," Mumbles Val, tearfully.

I hustle over to my house to grab some vodka from the back of my
cabinet, glad Roni and Val left it untouched. I hope Roni still has
those orange sodas in her fridge since I have nothing to mix them
with.

And then it hits me.

Val wanted me there.

Not just Roni.

Val, grieving for their grandmother, wanted me there for comfort.

Warmth radiates through my body as my heart pounds.

Holy cow.

I want to throw a party and tell everyone I'm accepted, but the reality of the situation hits before I start dancing a little jig.

Dead grandmother.

Get it together.

I let myself into Roni's place, make sure the house is locked up for the night, find the orange sodas and glasses, and head back to the bedroom. Roni is lying on her back with Val curled around her. Roni looks at me and smiles, love and gratitude in her eyes, and then Val notices the alcohol and scrambles to sit up, "Oh, bless you, Quinnie-pie. I need to forget. I'll fill y'all in tomorrow. Quinn, you can't work tomorrow. I need you here."

"Anything for you," I say, setting everything on the dresser and getting to work mixing the drinks like the excellent third wheel I am. I hand the bed folks their drinks and go into Roni's game closet, finding Cards Against Humanity, holding it behind my back as I return to the bedroom.

"Okay, y'all. This might be super inappropriate, and if it is, I'm sorry, but..." and I pull it out from behind my back.

Val squeals and says, "Oh. My. Glob. Yes, please. Oh, Quinn, I knew I needed you and Roni tonight."

Roni looks at me, head tilted to the side, eyes shining, and mouths, "Thank you." To which I send her a hopefully roguish wink. Trying to cover the fact that I almost can not contain my joy at being a part of their world. The way her expression turns to a smirk as she reaches out for the cards tells me I failed. I let her and Val get the game set up as I grab a folding table from the porch and set it up beside the bed to hold the drinks and snacks and all the things that could cause a mess.

We play, taking a drink every time we're shocked by a card, which is often. It doesn't take long before we slur our words while laughing too hard at the cards.

"And I would have gotten away with it, too, if it hadn't been for..." I say, laughing. A few seconds later, Val screeches, "Firing a rifle in the air while balls deep in a squealing hog!" and Roni shrieks, "What the actual hell?" and takes a huge gulp, along with Val and I. Everything is fuzzy; we're laughing hysterically, occasionally crying, and when my alarm goes off at 5 AM, I shoot what I hope is a coherent text to my foreman, letting him know I won't be in today.

Roni and Val have slowly settled into the bed, Beauty Shop playing on the tablet, and I squeeze in with them, my eyes heavy.

The bedside clock reads 3:00, and judging from the light coming in from the window, I assume that means 3 PM or something super weird is happening. My ass, hips, and legs are numb. I was sleeping propped up in a sitting position against the pillows, my legs spread wide, with Roni and Val clutching each other, sleeping with their heads on my thigh. I have a gnarly headache. My mouth is dry, and I will piss myself if I don't get to the bathroom soon. But, my goodness, I don't want to wake them.

I reach down and try to roll them off of my leg and fling my other leg over their bodies and end up flinging myself off the bed and onto the floor with a thud. Damn it; my entire lower body is waking up, spiky tingles breaking out and becoming practically unbearable. Shit, shit, shit.

When my body feels like my body again, I look at Roni and Val, glad to know they're still passed out and didn't witness my graceful exit. After taking care of my most urgent needs, I text Roni's family group chat, letting them know the situation and asking if they could bring us some Waffle House so I can wake my Roni and her Val with breakfast. After the confirmation, I walk over to my house, grab a few electrolyte drinks and my extra-strength Tylenol, down a couple, and chug a drink. I bring the rest over to Roni's. After stocking the refrigerator with my haul, I get to work making coffee and washing the few dishes Roni has. The last thing she needs to focus on is cleaning when Val needs her so much. I roam around, picking up tea cups, straightening blankets, and watering the plants that need it. Soon enough, my phone buzzes with a text letting me know Brian's outside with breakfast.

I head out, meeting Brian on the front porch, his arms loaded with Waffle House.

"How're they holding up?"

"Well, Val showed up in the middle of the night sobbing and we got totally shit-faced and now Roni and them are passed out in bed."

"Damn, going to be a hard morning. Glad you texted. You need me to get the gals over here?"

"I don't know yet. Let me wake them up and feed them. I'll shoot you a message."

"Whatever y'all need. We got you."

"Thanks."

I go back inside, weighed down with what feels like everything Waffle House sells, and start setting the food up on the table. I hear movement in the bedroom, grab the painkillers and a couple of electrolyte drinks, and then check on my people. Roni is half awake, leaning against the headboard with Val curled up in her lap. She gives me a bleary smile, and noticing my haul, she mouths, 'Thank you' as I lean over to kiss her.

I whisper, "We should probably wake them. Brian brought breakfast, and I'm sure we have a funeral to plan."

She nods, takes the Tylenol, chugs half the drink, and then rubs Val's back. Val slowly wakes up and sits up, eyes growing watery as the previous day washes over them.

"What time is it?" They croak as I hand them a drink and pills.

"Just after three," I say, gesturing for them to take the medication. I watch as they do and then take both drinks from them, helping them out of bed.

"Brian brought us breakfast and said to let the family know if we need anything."

Val's eyes fill with tears, "I love your family, Roni."

"Oh shush," Roni says, "They're your family, too"

This only makes Val cling to Roni and cry harder.

After a few minutes and a helpless look from Roni, I clap my hands together and say, "Val, if you're going to cry, you need to eat first, replenish your energy or something. Besides that, Waffle House is pretty gross cold, so we need to eat fast."

Val chuckles tearfully, "Thank you, Quinnie-pie."

While we eat, we discuss funeral arrangements and devise a game plan to make this as easy as possible for Val. Roni's siblings will handle everything not involving Memaw's last wishes, while Roni, Val, and I handle the rest.

The next couple of days are filled with funeral plans and cuddling Val through this whole ordeal. They're holding up so well, but the nights are really hard for them, so they've been sleeping in between Roni and me as if they're a child having a nightmare. Roni keeps apologizing, telling me that with their Memaw dead, we are the closest thing to family that Val has.

Finally I tell her, "Sunflower, I've already told you and I will tell you again. I love you, you love Val and as such, anything that they need, I am here for. Anything that you love is mine to take care of. I knew from the get-go that you and Val were a package deal, and it is a deal I would happily take again and again. Please, stop apologizing. I want to be here for them. I want them happy and safe. If that means sharing a bed with them forever, then you and I will have to get creative, but I don't mind."

"I just don't want you to resent me or Val or feel put out. I-"

Unable to bear her distress, I pull her to me. "I will never feel put out or resentful about your family. We might not be married, but your family is my family now. I need you to listen to the words coming out of my mouth. I love you. I love anyone that you love. I want to take care of you. I want to take care of anyone that you love. Please, believe me, you are my everything." Roni still looks like she might burst into tears at any time, and it occurs to me it's been at least a week since she's had her alone time. No wonder she is so insecure. Her brain gets all muddled when she's been overwhelmed by people for too long.

"Sunflower, I think you need some time alone. How about I take Val to get funeral clothes, and you stay here? Read, watch a movie, you could even go over to my house and veg out in front of the big TV."

"I couldn't do that to you. I need to take care of Val."

"And I need to take care of you. You need time alone to recharge. The funeral is tomorrow, and that is a lot of peopling. Take this afternoon so that you can be comfortable tomorrow."

"Are you sure?"

"Of course I am. It was my idea."

"Oh my goodness, thank you. You're right. I need it. It's just so hard to let go, to let you take care of my responsibilities."

"They're our responsibilities. Now, you go on inside and do whatever you need to do. I'll grab Val, and we'll be out of your hair." I say, slapping her on the ass.

I walk into the living room and find Val lying on the sofa, reading a battered paperback.

"Okay, Valley-Walley. You and I are going shopping, and Roni is going to be alone for a little while." I say, grinning down at them.

Their expression immediately turns to panic as they shoot up to stand. "Oh, my god. I am so sorry. I've overstayed my welcome. I am so sorry, I'll get Jackson to come pick me up. I'm sorry."

I grab their shoulders. "Hey, hey. Calm down. You are welcome to move in if you need to. Probably my house, since Roni needs her alone time, but still. You could never overstay your welcome. You know how Roni is. She needs time to recharge her batteries. You need funeral clothes. I'm great at carrying shit. So go grab your stuff and run over to my house and get ready to go. I'm going to run to the gas station and get Roni some snacks, and then you and me are going on an adventure."

"Are you sure?" They ask, their eyes still glassy.

"Of course. Now go."

Roni

When Quinn and Val leave, I just kind of roam around my place. Unable to decide if I want to watch a movie or read, but I need a cup of tea. Humming to myself, I start the kettle and gather my supplies. While it steeps, I decide to read a little, something cute. The front door creaks open just as I'm sitting down on my back porch, boots stomping through the house in my direction. I hop up, worried that Val isn't ok, only to see Quinn's smiling face through my back door.

"Everything is just fine, Sunflower," Quinn says, pulling me into his arms after tossing a bag in a chair.

"Then why are you back already?" I mumble into his chest, just breathing him in.

"I stopped by the gas station to get you some candy and a soda. You should have your snacks after all that you've done this week."

"I love you," I say, my face still mushed into his chest, his strong arms holding me tight.

"I love you, too," Quinn says, kissing my forehead in a sweet gesture that is quickly ruined when he slaps my ass, kisses my mouth, and just walks out the door.

I dig through my bag of sour gummy goodness and curl up on my porch papasan, getting all cozy to read my silly little book.

Quinn

My heart warm, I stroll over to my house to wait on Val. They are walking into my living room, ready to go. Val's eyes are rimmed in red and their face is bare of all makeup. They are wearing one of my way too big for them t-shirts and an ankle-length green skirt from Roni. It bums me out to see them anything less than their usual extravagantly put-together self. I snatch them up in a big bear hug and ask, "You want to ride up to the Wal-Mart or head to Spanish Fort?"

"Oh, Wal-Mart is fine. I don't want to put you out too much." Val mumbles against my chest.

Oh, hell no.

I gently push them back so I can look straight into Val's striking blue eyes, "I'm going to tell you like I told Roni. I adore Roni. More than life itself. And anything or anyone that Roni loves I love. Anything that Roni would do for you, I am willing to do for you. You are not a burden. I'll take you all the way to Mobile or Pensacola if you want, but I just figured we could find the same sad black clothes in this county. But it's up to you, you hear me? I am at your beck and call."

They sniff tearfully and blink back a stray tear saying, "Wal-Mart really is fine. I doubt I will ever want to wear the clothes again after the funeral, anyways."

"Alrighty-then. Let's do this."

I should have taken Val to any place other than the Bay Minette Wal-Mart. Holy Cow. We can't take three steps without someone offering Val condolences. Somehow, we manage to find a couple of sad black dresses for Val and wander over to the food side, looking for snacks to sustain us until Roni decides to feed us. They've changed the damn layout of the grocery aisles again, and we make a wrong turn down the canned food aisle.

"Ooooh! Spaghetti-Os!" Val exclaims, "My Memaw used to buy these for me."

I watch in horror as their eyes fill with tears right here in front of canned pasta. I quickly grab a few cans of the childhood favorite and toss them in the buggy.

"Well, it looks like we are having Spaghetti-Os today!" I say as cheerfully as possible which only manages to make their tears actually fall.

"I can't," they cry, "It won't be the same without my Memaw to make them for me."

"I'm your Memaw now and I'll make you canned Spaghetti-Os whenever you need them." I say, hoping for a smile.

I get something better: a giggle from them as they say, "That actually sounds great, Memaw Quinn."

I ruffle their hair and chuckle, "Roni is never going to let me live this down."

"Nope," Val says, popping the p.

Roni

I must have dozed off because the sun is much lower in the sky and my book is on the floor. There is also a Sour Patch Kid tangled in my hair, good thing it didn't melt or something. I clean up my little mess of spilled candy and grab my book off the floor, making my way back inside. I glance out my front window to see if Quinn's truck is here, and it is. I wonder what he and Val are up to.

I decide to walk over there to see what they want for dinner. Flinging open Quinn's door, I am horrified at what I see before me.

Quinn and Val, my two favorite people on earth, are sitting cross-legged on the floor in front of the TV, watching anime, and eating Spaghetti-Os like heathens.

"What is this? Ruining y'alls dinner with Spaghetti-Os? Seriously, those nasty things?"

"You take that back! I used to eat these with Memaw when I was little! I just wanted a taste!" Val says, eyes watering. Damn it.

"I'm sorry, I didn't realize. I thought Quinn had coerced you into eating junk food with him," I say, wrapping myself around Val as they giggle through their tears.

"Hey! I would never do that!" Quinn says, chuckling.

"Sure you wouldn't," I say, smirking at him. He laughs and leans over, takes Val's bowl from them, and sits it on the floor. He then wraps his arms around the both of us in a squeezing bear hug.

When Quinn loosens his grip, I lean back to look at Val and say, "Did you have enough of a taste? Or is this your dinner?"

They sniffle, then sigh, and say, "No, a taste was enough. They really are nasty. Kids have horrible taste in pasta."

Quinn gasps and picks up Val's bowl, shoveling the last bite into his mouth. "This stuff is so good, y'all are crazy."

The sun shines brightly the next day as we leave the funeral home, Memaw's ashes in Val's lap. We took Quinn's truck with all three of us up front on his bench seat so Val could sit between us. Their head rests on my shoulders with my arms surrounding them, their hand clutching Quinn's dress shirt, as if afraid to let either of us go.

They insist we take them back home. That they want to be alone, to truly grieve. I don't like it but Quinn reminded me it isn't my choice.

We pull up to the farm and Quinn gets out first, walking around to open my door and help me and Val out of the truck. Val hugs me tight, and whispers, "Thank you," then we feel Quinn's strong arms surrounding us.

"Okay, okay, I'm being suffocated in love. I'm fine. Going to go lay in Memaw's bed, sob, and then get back to life."

I feel my eyes well with tears. "Do you want me to stay with you?"

Val says, "Nope. I need to be alone."

"Okay. Okay. Love you."

"Love you, too."

Quinn then boops Val's nose and says, "We are only a phone call away. You don't have to do anything alone unless you want to."

And now both Val and I have tears streaming down our faces.

"Thanks, Quinn. Now you both have to go."

Chapter 33
Kissing under dinosaurs.

Roni

"**S**ugar-Bear, take me to Bamahenge on your bike," I demand as I watch him finish hanging a new shelf in my living room. He chuckles as he finishes packing his battered red toolbox and sits beside me on my purple sofa.

"I'll take you anywhere you want to go, Sunflower, but what the hell is a Bamahenge?"

"Okay, so it'll take us about an hour and a half to get there. There's a lifesize replica of Stonehenge made of fiberglass, four huge dinosaurs, and a giant metal spider. Oh! And a sundial and other things hidden in the woods all along the roadside. And my absolute favorite part is the lady in the lake. She is massive and made of fiberglass and lives in the marina. They pull her out during hurricane season but hopefully, she is out there now." I'm practically bouncing in my seat, the thought of a long ride and seeing the lady in the lake distracting me from Quinn until he reaches across the couch and pulls me into his lap.

Laughing, I squeal, "Quinn!"

Peppering kisses all over my face, Quinn laughs and bear hugs me. I squeeze him back just as tightly, enjoying the pressure and the tickle of his beard. Sometimes, it feels like he is the only thing holding my pieces together.

"Alright, Sugar Tits, get jeans and boots on, and we'll head out. Want to stop for lunch or pack something?" Quinn says with a smirk.

I bark out a laugh, "Sugar Tits? You better not call me that in front of folks."

"I would never. Now, what about food?"

"I don't want to make anything, so you pick us a restaurant. I want to go to a sit-down, not fast food." I say, climbing off his lap.

"Let's go to Lamberts!" He says rather excitedly.

"I love their rolls, but I hate having to catch them. I always end up dropping like three on the ground."

"Don't worry, babe. I'll catch your rolls for you," He says, smiling indulgently at me.

"Deal."

Quinn

I'm sitting on my bike when Roni comes running out of her house, her wild hair contained in two braids, wearing baggy jeans with little flowers all over them, an orange tank top, and a huge smile that makes my heart stutter. She abruptly stops and says, "Damn it, forgot my jacket. I'll be right back."

"Hold up, Sunflower. Check the saddlebag. I got you a present."

"Oooh, really?" She says, wiggling her hips as she pulls out a shimmery orange helmet and a black bag. She squeals and practically throws the black bag in my face as she gives me a huge smacking kiss and shoves the helmet on.

"I love it so much! It is perfect!"

"And that is only half of it. Take a look in the bag," I say, laughing with her as she snatches the bag from my hands and pulls out a buttery soft leather jacket. She hugs it to her chest and jumps up and down.

"Quinn Eugene Evans! I love it!"

I chuckle and pull her to me for a kiss. She pulls back from me and flips the jacket over, sighing a huge, melodramatic sigh while looking at the back.

"What's the matter, babe?" I ask, wondering what she is up to.

"I was expecting to see 'Property of Quinn' or something on the back." My Sunflower pouts.

"I'm not in a motorcycle club, Roni."

"You could be. It would be so cool."

"I'll consider your request," I say as I buckle Roni's shimmery orange helmet and kiss her on the nose. A magical giggle rings out, making my heart pound.

She slings her leg over the back of my Harley, and I reach behind me to grab her legs and pull her as close to me as possible. I've never had a woman who wanted to ride around with me, and Roni's love of riding further proves she's the one for me. The slight chill in the air and the heat from Roni against my back are perfect as we take off.

The ride through the woods and into town was amazing, especially since it isn't tourist season and the roads aren't crowded. We stop at Lambert's Cafe first since it is right after lunchtime, and we are seated in the rustic restaurant right away.

"I think this is the first time this place hasn't had a long wait," Roni says after the hostess seats us.

"I'm glad. Don't think I could wait too long. I'm starving."

She laughs, "You're always starving."

I wiggle my eyebrows at her and say, "Only for you, Sunflower."

She lightly blushes as she giggles and says, "Oh hush, you dreadful man."

A server wearing red suspenders comes by with an enormous bowl. "Y'all want some fried okra to start you off?"

"Oh, yes, please!" Roni says as I tear off some paper towels so he can dump the okra. He winks at Roni before he walks away, causing a sliver of jealousy to run down my spine when she giggles.

That magical giggle is mine, damn it.

Roni, her mouth full of fried okra, notices my change in mood. She nudges me over and over until she's able to swallow her food.

"You can't be jealous." She says, looking at me thoughtfully.

"Of course I can. He winked at you, and you giggled. You're only supposed to giggle at me."

She leans over and lays her head on my shoulder. "I'll never giggle at another man again."

"You better not, woman," I say, pulling her chin up for a quick kiss.

"I promise. Now, catch me a roll, will you? I see the molasses lady coming around."

"As you wish."

Quinn

I slow my bike as we turn down the road to the marina and keep going slow so Roni can find the hidden goodies out here. She taps me on the side, pointing to the right at a little gravel parking area that can fit maybe five cars. Roni is off the bike before I can help her, bouncing and chattering about the area's history. She grabs my hand, making my heart skip a beat as it always does, and drags me down a trail surrounded by woods. In a clearing up ahead is Stonehenge. You don't realize how tall those suckers are until you are standing beside them. They look realistic until you get right up close. Roni pulls her camera out of her purple crossbody bag and directs me to stand beside one of those towering things, making silly faces at me until I crack up, and she snaps her Polaroid. She then convinces a teenager to take our photo with Bamahenge in the background. This magical woman then grabs my hand and pulls me along the side of the road and to another trail into the woods. We reach the end of the path to find a T-Rex towering over us.

Roni sets her camera on a low-hanging tree branch and pushes a couple of buttons before running over to me, grabbing my face, and kissing me. The camera clicks, and I continue kissing her. She giggles against my mouth, my magical giggle, and whispers, "I love you."

Ah, fuck, this woman owns my heart.

"I love you, too, my Sunflower."

She wiggles out of my arms, dances over to her camera, and retrieves the photo of us kissing under the dinosaur.

"I'm going to have to start a whole wall of Polaroids of us," she says, grabbing my hand and pulling me back towards my bike. "Or I could take down my other photo wall and transfer those to a scrapbook."

My heart races at the thought of her wanting to trade her travel photo wall for me.

"Just let me know what you need me to do, hot stuff. A photo wall of us sounds nice. We've definitely taken enough pictures." I say, trying to contain my excitement. She might be fiercely independent but she sure does want me.

When we reach the bike, she tells me that farther down the road are a couple more dinosaurs, under which we take more kissing pictures. She then directs me to the marina to find this lady in the water.

We drive past a huge fountain and a giant spider to park in front of a pier. Roni squeals as she yanks off of her helmet and tries to jump off the bike, managing to get her foot stuck in the saddlebag. She would have busted her ass if I hadn't snatched her around the waist, almost toppling me and the bike in the process.

"The lady in the lake is here! Look!" She says excitedly. I look where her finger points and see a massive woman's head and knees poking out of the water. I can see why Roni is so enamored; the lady would probably be twenty stories high if she stood up. Sunflower has her Polaroid hanging from her neck and is snapping pictures on her phone while bouncing around and chattering about how the lady ended up in this particular lake. I walk behind her and pull her back to my front, kissing the side of her head. She reaches up and pats my cheek, pushes away from me to set up her camera on the railing, and sets the timer before skipping to me. I yank her against me, dip her, and press my lips to hers just as we hear the click. Her magical giggle wraps around us, and she says, "I bet that was the best one yet!"

With my hand in hers, I walk up to the railing, where she grabs the picture and shakes it. "It's beautiful! This one is going to go front and center on my new photo wall!"

Quinn

I'm dozing in my recliner, a bowl of popcorn resting on my stomach. Roni wanted to be alone tonight after our little adventure yesterday, so I'm on my own for the night.

"Quinn Eugene Evans!" Roni bellows, flinging open my front door, as she always does. My heart skips a beat at seeing her smiling face, her excitement palpable. She's wearing one of my t-shirts that hangs down to her knees and I just know she isn't wearing anything underneath. She never does.

"What's up, Sunflower?" I ask as I pull her to me for a kiss, sliding my hands under the shirt to grab her bare ass.

"The lightning bugs are out! Let's go watch them!" She practically squeals.

"Alright, let me go get some pants on," I say, gesturing to my hot pink boxer briefs.

"No time! What if we miss them? You rarely see them anymore!"

I chuckle as I snag the blanket Roni demanded I keep on the back of my sofa, toss her over my shoulder with a slap on her bare ass, and let her magical giggle wash over me. I walk her over to the backyard and see the treeline twinkling like the stars against the sky. I slowly slide her down my front, gripping her butt as my lips meet hers. She smiles against my lips, palms on my cheeks, "I love you, Sugar-Bear." I chuckle, remembering a time when she couldn't say the words, but I could feel them etched on my soul.

"I love you, too, Sunflower."

She giggles and says, "We sound like a children's book, Sunflower and the Sugar-Bear!"

"What about Sugar-Bear and the Sunflower? About a bear that finds the most precious sunflower and takes care of her for the rest of his life?"

Her eyes turn dreamy, the fireflies glittering, as she smiles, "That's perfect. As long as he stays in his cave and lets the sunflower stay in her field."

Barking out a laugh, I fling the blanket on the ground and pull her to sit in between my legs, facing the trees. She gently trails her fingers up and down my bare thighs, tickling me a little. I lightly slap at her hands, saying, "Hey now, that tickles."

"That's the point." She says, her voice laced with laughter as she digs her fingers in a little harder. I flip her around, tickling her ribs, listening to her beautiful snort-laugh ring out. I keep tickling her as payback until she's laughing and squealing, "I'm going to pee, Quinn! Stop!" Not wanting to see that, I stop and lean over her, taking her mouth in a kiss that quickly ends our laughter as it turns passionate. She sighs into my mouth as I deepen the kiss, ravaging her mouth. She runs her hands up my chest and into the hair at the nape of my neck, sending sparks everywhere she touches. I pull her up to yank my shirt over her head, her magical giggle ringing out at my eagerness. She matches my energy, tugging my boxers down so I can kick them off. I roll us so that she is on top, taking one of her nipples in my mouth. I tug and tease each one until she is frantically moaning and grinding on me, her wetness rubbing up and down my hard cock. Her whimpered begging has me sliding down until her gorgeous pussy is right over my mouth. "Sit on my face, baby," I growl, shoving a finger inside of her. She lowers herself slightly, barely close enough to get a taste. I slap her ass and grab her hips, pulling her down as I snarl, "I said. Sit on my face, woman, not hover. I want to drown in you."

She sobs out my name as I feast, two fingers pumping, my mouth on her clit. Her legs shake as I add a third finger, her juices coating my beard, yelling out her orgasm.

I immediately flip her over, hands and knees, and shove into her, thrusting wildly into the woman I adore. Grabbing her swinging tits, I tug her sensitive nipples, causing her pussy to tighten on my cock. I reach down and slap her clit, once, twice, making her gasp and thrust back harder, and when I pinch her little bud, she lets loose, screaming out her second orgasm. I follow right behind her with a bellow, my god, she is incredible. Flopping to the side, I pull her in to cuddle under the fireflies bugs.

"I love you," She says, her lips on my neck.

"I love you, too, and I always will."

We lay there in her backyard, cuddled up and naked, until long after the fireflies went to bed.

Chapter 34
Wanted: A Part-Time Husband

Roni

I'm in the middle of a work project when a knock on my front door startles me. Not expecting anyone I peer out of the living room window, and once I see Quinn, I fling open the door. He is standing on my front porch, covered in grime from work, holding a bouquet of wildflowers with a large grin.

"Sugar-Bear! Why didn't you just come in?"

"I'm here to ask you for a date, and I wanted to do it right," he says, handing me the flowers.

"Well, sir, come on in while I settle these flowers in a vase. They are beautiful, by the way. I love them."

He follows me into the kitchen, leans against the doorjamb, and smiles softly while watching me flutter around the kitchen. I sit the gorgeous flowers in the center of my old table and then place my hands on his chest, leaning in for a kiss. After a couple of minutes,

Quinn smacks my ass and says, "Stop distracting me, woman. Now back up so I can do this right."

I giggle and do as he asks.

"That's better. Now, my dearest Veronica, would you do me the honor of accompanying me to dinner tonight at Grace's Steakhouse?" He asks, grabbing my hands and kissing my knuckles.

"Of course I will."

He pumps his fist like he's freeze-framed in an 80s movie while I laugh at his antics. He yanks me to him, crushing his lips to mine. I melt into the kiss, my heart pounding. Way too soon, he pulls back kissing my forehead.

"Okay, go get ready. I have to shower and all that."

"I'll see you in a couple of hours, handsome."

He wiggles his eyebrows. One more kiss, and he's out the door, jogging through the yard and into his house.

I plan to take my time getting ready. I so rarely wear makeup that if I'm not careful, I will screw it up. I video-call Val for help with winged eyeliner.

"Help!" I yell as soon as they pick up.

"With what?" They yell back.

"Quinn asked me out on a fancy date, so I want to do winged eyeliner. Walk me through it, please." I say, mildly panicked and waving a liquid liner pen around.

"Okay, the first thing is to put that liquid liner down. You'll just fuck that up. Why would you even have that? Nevermind. Find a pencil liner."

"This one?" I ask, holding up a different liner.

"That'll do. Now, do you have a teensy angled brush? Look in that kit I gave you."

"This?"

"Smaller," they say.

After rummaging for a few seconds, I hold up the only other option, "This is the smallest one in the pack."

"That one is perfect."

An hour and twelve makeup wipes later, Val says, "Holy shit. You look freaking hot. Like, you are gorgeous, but with this Marylin Monroe red lip and eyeliner combo, damn. If Quinn actually takes you out looking that hot, I will be so surprised."

"Oh, he is going to take me out. I spent way too much time on this look to not show it off," I laugh.

"Guess it's his turn to watch you get hit on right in front of his face. What are you wearing? Something tiny?"

"I don't think I have anything tiny. But I planned on the black dress with the slit up to almost my hip and those new stilettos we bought last shopping trip."

"Oh, that's even better than tiny. Classy sexy. Send me a photo of you and Quinn. Bet y'all are going to be so freaking cute tonight."

"Will do."

I hear Quinn's knock on the door as I slide on my shoes. I fling open the door, strike a pin-up pose, and watch Quinn's jaw hit the floor.

"Like what you see, big boy?" I ask, smirking.

"Holy shit, Sunflower. I love what I see. Come here and give me your lips," He says, reaching to the back of my neck and pulling me to him. When we pull away from each other, Quinn's mouth is smeared with red lipstick. He looks baffled as I giggle. Before he figures it out, I pull my phone out of my wristlet and pull him in for a selfie. As soon as he sees his face, he laughs. I take him into the bathroom, where he washes his face, and I fix my smudged lipstick. I pull us in front of the full length to take our photo.

Quinn looks so handsome in his gray suit with a striped tie, and I send the picture to Val. I might include the smeared lipstick photo, too.

When they immediately reply, I tell Quinn, "Val says you look very handsome and that they love that shade of lipstick on you."

He chuckles, smirking, "Good. I'll probably end up wearing it for most of the night."

"Should I go take it off? I want our date to be fun, not fussy, you know?"

"Leave it on. I want to see it smeared around my cock later."

I gasp, "Oh my god, Quinn!"

He chuckles, "Let's go, sexy lady."

Quinn holds my hand as we walk to his truck, and he helps me in. Sitting on the armrest between the seats is a little iridescent gift bag. "Oh, Sugar-Bear! A gift?"

He slaps my hand away, "Yes, but not yet. Don't ruin my surprise."

"I don't like surprises."

"You'll like this one."

"We'll see," I say, scowling.

He grins down at me, buckles my seatbelt, and kisses my forehead. "Patience, my love."

I stick my tongue out at him, and he laughs, grabbing the tip. I jerk back, laughing, and tilt my face for a light kiss.

Soon enough, we pulled into the restaurant parking lot, his hand on my thigh and laughter wrapped around us.

"Sit tight," Quinn says, kissing the back of my hand. He grabs the gift bag, jumps out of the truck, and hustles around to help me out.

"If this hostess hits on you, do you want me to fist-fight her? Because I will." I say, laughing as Quinn takes my hand and leads me toward the restaurant entrance.

"Nah, babe, I can't see any woman but you, so it doesn't matter who hits on me. But damn, it's so hot that you would defend my honor." He says as the host holds open the door for us.

"All day, every day," I say smiling up at him.

He winks at me before turning to the host and saying, "Reservations under Quinn Evans, please."

"Yes, sir. Right this way," He says, leading us to a candle-lit table in the corner. It's perfect, pristine white tablecloth and the illusion of privacy with the dimmed lighting.

"Oh, Quinn. This is so romantic, thank you." I say as he helps me into my chair and sits across from me.

He grabs my hand, "It's a very special day for me. I want it to always be romantic for you."

A sliver of panic runs through me that I forgot his birthday or something. Before I can spiral into negative thoughts, Quinn squeezes my hand, kisses my knuckles, and says, "Don't worry, you haven't forgotten anything. Even though today is a very important day. One of the most important ones in my life."

"Will you tell me what it is or do I have to guess? Please don't make me guess, I suck at this game."

Quinn laughs and says, "I'm not going to make you guess. Open your surprise."

I make grabby hands for the gift bag and Quinn chuckles, handing me the bag. I pull out a small purple frame, the same color as my sofa, with a newspaper cut out. I look at Quinn, confused, but my eyes fill with tears as I start to read.

My original social media post begging for a part-time husband is right here, in my hands, typed up and printed to look like a wanted ad.

Wanted: A Part-Time Husband

Duties: Lawn care, general home maintenance, light plumbing, and all other "husband jobs"

Payment: Home-cooked meals and a clean house.

Look, I don't want to take care of my house. I want a single man with commitment issues to take care of all of the things I don't want to do when it comes to my house. In exchange, I will feed you and clean your house.

"It's beautiful," I say, eyes watery, looking at Quinn's precious face.

"Exactly one year ago today, I read these exact words and thought, 'Damn, I want all the home-cooked meals.' but I never imagined that you would completely change my life. I love you so much, Sunflower. I will be grateful that you hate owning a home until the day that I die."

"And I will be grateful that you are always hungry. I love you, Sugar-Bear."

Epilogue
9 Months Later

Quinn

I slap my hand on Roni's thigh, squeezing it, and say, "Well, sexy lady, what are we celebrating tonight?"

"It's a surprise!" She chirps, jiggling the gift bag she won't let me look in.

"I hate surprises."

"Shut up. No, you don't."

"Yeah, yeah. Sit tight," I say, kissing the back of her hand. I climb out of the truck and hurry around to help my lady out. Once I have her hand back in mine, we walk into Grace's Steakhouse. Roni looks amazing tonight, wearing a knee-length, deep red dress, black high heels, and sexy hair piled high on her head, with pieces caressing her cheeks and neck. Sometimes, it is hard to breathe; she's so beautiful.

The hostess leads us to the same candle-lit table where Roni and I spent our anniversary. Roni's eyes are sparkling and full of mischief, and she can barely contain her excitement as I help her into the seat. Our server walks up just as I sit down, and we order water as we peruse the menu. Ages ago, we agreed not to drink on dates so that we could clearly remember all of our special moments.

"Ready to give me my surprise, Sunflower?"

She grins at me and bounces in her seat just a little bit. "Yes! I wanted to wait until after we ate, but I just can't! I just want you to know how much I love you. It was hard for me to really trust that being in love was enough, but one year ago today, you proved how much you loved me and how much you will sacrifice for me. And that was what I needed to accept that you and I, and our two houses and Ginger, are it, forever. That's why, every single day of my life, I wear this ring around my neck. To always have you close to my heart, just where you belong."

As if she didn't just decimate me, she giggles and hands me the gift bag. I can't do anything but stare at her gorgeous face, reliving the last couple of years together until she snaps her fingers in front of my face and says, "Earth to Quinn, you okay there, Sugar-Bear?"

I laugh, "Sorry, Sunflower."

She smiles and bounces as she waits for me to open her gift. As soon as I pull out the simple wooden frame with a newspaper clipping, I can not control my laughter.

This woman has framed my damn mugshot.

Somehow, here in this fancy restaurant, holding a framed clipping of my mugshot, I fall even more in love with Roni.

Epilogue 2
10 Years Later

Quinn

"Hey, babe, what do you want to do for our anniversary?" I ask as we sit at my kitchen table to eat the takeout that I picked up on the way home from work. Just two more years and I can retire. Roni has so many travel plans for us that I'm starting to wonder if I'll be able to keep up with her. My thoughts spiral down the rabbit hole of who will replace me when I retire and if I can convince my girl that we need a huge, fancy bus to haul us all over the country.

"I want you to fuck me in the ass for our anniversary."

"Okay, babe. I'll get to it after I do the dishes." I say absentmindedly as I spear another green bean on my fork. Slowly, the words that came out of her mouth make connections in my slow as fuck brain. My heart races and my blood is pounding in my veins. She didn't say...

"Wait, what?" I ask with more force than necessary, looking at her embarrassed face.

"I want you to fuck me in the ass." She says, looking at the table.

My jaw drops in shock, and my dick gets so hard, so fast, that it's painful. Fuck, a fifty-three-year-old cock shouldn't be able to rise this fast. But I've been wanting that ass for years and this feels like the best thing that's ever happened to me.

Well, outside of just Roni, anyway. She's the best thing.

But that ass, I have to bite my fist to keep from growling or something just as cheesy. Somewhere around year three, I asked to fuck her ass. She declined, said maybe another time. So every year on our anniversary, I would ask for her ass as a gift, and every year, she would laugh and turn me down.

But this year, oh fuck, this year.

I hear that magical giggle of hers, the one that enchanted me from our very first meeting, and look at her. My lover. She's watching me with a smirk and I realize I must have really zoned out.

"Shit, baby. You had to tell me at dinner? I'm so hard right now that I could hammer nails with my dick." She snort-laughs at that, but then her face gets serious, and she says, "Well, why don't you come over here and...nail me with that hammer?"

Hell yeah.

Epilogue 3
40 Years Later

Quinn

What is that god-awful noise waking me up? Well, fuck, it's my damn phone. That I left on the other side of the bedroom. My shoulder creaks as I try to rotate the knots out of it like the doctor showed me. It's been acting up more than usual, Roni's probably going to make me go back to the doctor soon.

"Okay, okay. I'm coming. Hold your horses," I say to my shrill phone, hobbling over to it. Seems to take forever to get my hips working right in the mornings.

Sunflower flashes on the screen and my heart skips a beat as I answer.

"Hello, my love. I thought it was your turn to wake me up in bed this morning?"

I hear her tearfully sigh before answering in a shaky voice, "Damn arthritis again. My knees hurt too bad to make it over this morning." She cries, breaking my heart.

"Give me a couple minutes, and I'll be right there."

I shower, shit, shave and brush my teeth in record time, eager to kiss the most beautiful woman in the world good morning. I change into my flannel lounge pants. We won't be leaving our property today, and slide into my slippers.

Memories of the last forty years wash over me. Our fifth-anniversary commitment ceremony, Roni wore a sexy wedding dress and we promised to love and never live together. The year we spent traveling the country after I retired. How Roni flings open my door and yells my middle name.

How my heart still skips a beat every time I hear her magical giggle.

It only takes a couple of minutes to get out of my door, through the yard, and into her side door. I walk back to her bedroom immediately climbing into bed and pulling her into my arms, taking my first full breath this morning "Hey, beautiful, decided to play princess and make me come to you, huh?" She gives a watery laugh and just squeezes my hand tighter. I kiss her temple, my heart still beating for her alone, and say, "Well, Sunflower, I think it's time that we move in together."

"Fine. But you better not put your balls on my couch." She says.

With Gratitude

To my husband, David, thank you. For everything. For more than I could ever express. Without you this book would have never have happened. You supported me, brought me sour candy and took care of me when I couldn't take care of myself.

To my Momma, thank you for always encouraging me and my whimsy. Your unwavering support means everything to me.

To V.H.Q. Blackstone, my very own personal Val. I owe this entire book to you. From the very first sentence to the last edit, you have been there. Laughing, critiquing, encouraging, editing: You did it all with me. Without your constant input and love for these characters I would have never finished this story.

About Lovey LaRue

Lovey LaRue is a romance author who believes every love story deserves a little sparkle. Married for almost 20 years and raising two teenagers, she finds inspiration in the beautiful, messy magic of everyday life. When she's not writing, you'll find her sipping tea with a good book, wandering mountain trails, or snuggling with her cat. With a giggle, a wink, and a dash of pink, she fills her stories with laughter, love, and shenanigans.

www.ingramcontent.com/pod-product-compliance
Lightning Source LLC
Chambersburg PA
CBHW010654100726
47901CB00012B/2538